Upside Book 2

Fort Brimat

©Peter M. EMMERSON 2020

This is a work of fantasy/science fiction. Names, characters, places and incidents either are the product of the author's imagination or are used fictitiously, and any resemblance to actual persons, living or dead, business establishments, events, or locales is entirely coincidental.

All rights reserved, including the right to reproduce this eBook or portions thereof in any form whatsoever.

This eBook is licensed for your personal enjoyment only.

This eBook may not be re-sold or given away to other people. If you would like to share this eBook with another person, please obtain an additional copy for each reader. If you're reading this eBook and did not purchase it, or it was not purchased or gifted for your use only, then please purchase your own copy.

If you enjoyed Book one of this Saga, mixing Sci Fi and Fantasy, thank you, but there's oodles more to come.

Fiction, Fantasy, Apocalyptic Themes, Dystopian Science Fiction

~

I'd like to mention all those who gave support through the six months of lock down but other than my wife Mary and stepson Darran, there weren't many from outside my bubble, who could spare the time.

Once again I must give a special word of thanks to my very busy Number 1 Beta reader, Jon Sherwood, for invaluable comments, corrections and suggestions.

Please provide some feedback/critique it's most appreciated, and it helps me to improve my writing.   Thank you --- Pete

WHAT HAS GONE BEFORE AND WHAT IS YET TO COME

Book One focused on the life, and frequently *the loves* of Rob Clitheroe, (after all how many red-blooded teenagers aren't continually thinking about *it*?...) 5,000 years is a long time for anything to survive, the underground city Castra is failing, Will its remaining inhabitants make their way to the surface, once there what will they find?

Book one continues with Rob's life on the Upside as a commander of a group of misfits tasked with reconnaissance. The Upside with its terrors and dangers, are not kind to Rob and his troopers. Finally he and the few survivors are rescued and adopted by the Clan Tirnano. Will Rob, who through destiny becomes the companion and rider of the Purple Queen of the M'ntar, joining with a smattering of Brosynans and the powerful Tirnano clan, be sufficient to face the Adversary and the Anakim giants?

~

And now for Book Two:

FORT BRIMAT

Book Two Introduces the arrival of The M'ntar. It continues by following the growth and revelations in the life of Q'rem, a young girl chosen at birth by Lord Dominie of the M'ntar to be his companion and rider.

Thrust into the aeon's long war between ancient gods. Q'rem with her mentor and guide Sekhi, a diminutive blonde, with fantastic powers and a hidden identity spend a time of revelation.

After undergoing incredible changes to his abilities, caused by his cerebral link with the Purple M'ntar Queen, Rob is suffering from strange side effects. Q'rem and Sekhi, join forces with Rob, his girls and the Purple Queen to combat the dark celestial powers that threaten to destroy their 'New' world.

FORT BRIMAT

I must begin with these extracts from my journal:
My name is Q'asha.(pronounced Kasha) I am an Elder of Fort Brimat, born of the line of the 'Rom Firster Max.' I am Keeper of the History Strips, Medic and Midwife. Our Ark had two factions when it was first populated almost five thousand years ago. Smokies and Rom, and although we integrated well, the Rom tried to keep their bloodlines pure, but over the years they blurred and finally combined.

Ancestry is important to all of us, and we carefully watch over our roots.

ONE THOUSAND THREE HUNDRED YEARS BEFORE THE SEEDING OF PLANET EARTH BY THE GREATER GODS, ANUBIS AND SEKHMET

Author's note: To assist with reader understanding, I have given Joe Kinnear and his log human like characteristics, obviously he is not human, nor has he any characteristics.

Although written in cursive script, it has never been translated... until now that is, for you are the first to read and understand it.

JOE KINNEAR

Joe Kinnear was an unfathomable person, not one given to outbursts or displays of enthusiasm. He was only happy when he was alone in deep space, and would have comfortably stayed there isolated from others, had it not been for the need to head planet side at least once a year to trade and replenish his stocks.

Kinnear was one of a group named The Travellers.

They spent their lives space hopping from populated planet to populated planet, in their beat-up ships to trade. They could all tell stories of travelling in random directions through the universe, in their old and most times dangerously converted cargo ships. The pilots, searching for that special something that would make them rich beyond imagination.

They lived either alone or with their entire families in their vessels; for the most part they had no planet side associations of any consequence. For them to disappear for many years, or even forever caused no real concern or heartache, for anyone left behind.

Kinnear's ship the Rambler, a cargo sloop, one time pride of the convoy route to Andora Base One. The Rambler had once held the dubious title of having the fastest Andora to Karinda crossing record, but that was before she had been fitted with YPL, now she could easily cross ten galaxies in less real time.

Kinnear traded as a repairer of metal articles, once upon a time he might have been known as a 'Tinker', with the Rambler as his horse and vardo. He had a small shuttle which he used to carry his 'wares' and himself, from ship to planet side whenever necessary, which as far as he was concerned was too often.

When he did stop, he would choose a recently colonised planet, sometimes to honestly do business, others times to trick the unwary or the stupid out of their belongings, depending on his mood at the time, and the vigilance of the local law enforcement agencies.

The explosion of the race was still in its infancy, no more than five hundred years had passed since that great exodus from the miserable, worn out and probably by now destroyed 'mother world'. Some of the planets which he and his fellows visited had not seen an off worlder from the day they were first colonised hundreds of years previously. There were sufficient colonised planets for him to visit a new one each week of his remaining life if he so chose.

Many planets held tightly to the strict codes of behaviour which they had carried with them from Andora, and did not take kindly to off worlders arriving and breaking rules.

On these planets Kinnear found it impossible to trade with people who hid away from him, or would force him to leave. On other occasaions he would endeavour to win the population round with his unique sideshow, bringing the inhabitants out of their hiding places, if that plan failed, which it sometimes did, he would leave and thereafter give those 'hermit' planets a wide berth.

Freedom to be *'whatever one chose to be'* was encouraged on many liberated planets, so long as it did not adversely affect others. This was their accepted way of life, and the one rigorously enforced rule which ran throughout most of their near and far outposts.

Most times, the Travellers were welcomed, bringing as they did news and information, new technological inventions, or medicinal advances and useful equipment to those far flung colonies.

The young colonies were stretched far apart, vast distances between them, each one, in spite of everything, in control of its own destiny. For the hub had not yet been formed, the hub which one day would be the centre of every universe, controlling and directing every planet that people stepped upon.

Free trade and enterprise was still welcomed on most planets, in those long ago days, for it was to be another eight hundred years before things would have changed beyond all reckoning.

The lives of those early colonists had been in the main hard, fighting to survive on off-times unpleasant planets, in many cases not where they had originally planned to go to, but planets where unscrupulous Cruiser captains had decided to drop them, rather than rummage about for the ideal utopias which their passengers dreamed of and had paid for.

Life on the whole was precious on those frontier planets, freedom too, but the respect for each other's right to privacy was the most important of all.

KINNEAR'S LOG

I had begun to tire of the metal walls of The Rambler. I had begun to dream of earth beneath my feet, I had begun to dream of a planet of my own, one where I could stop my travelling and settle down to live and die in the peace and solitude I have always craved.

To be able to breathe fresh air, not air that that has been recycled through my ship's filters a million times, but most of all I yearn for a planet where I would be undisturbed by the noise, the clutter, the lusts and the stupidity of other creatures like myself.

In my search for my own private haven, I began to aim my computers in hit and miss directions, leaving the machines to take me wherever they would. It was not long before I had passed a long way outside the normal trade routes taken by the Space cruisers which travelled between the more densely populated planets, the planets were situated around the centres of the ten home universes and which had formed our infant coalition federation.

I began to spend months of travelling in sub hyper (just below the speed of light) re-orientating myself to the whereabouts of my random destinations, when I came out of suspension. I lost count of the many times I was disappointed at not finding a perfect planet.

I would then re-program my computers to return me to a more populated part of the universe, to trade for more provisions, and then once again fire myself across the galaxy, in search of my utopia on the opposite side.

It was on one of those times of drifting when a howl from my long range scanners broke into my sleep period, a howl which warned me of the proximity of a potentially suitable star system, the crisp, static feel of the air indicated that YPL was active, and even though it was operating at its lowest power level, at minimum speed, I would still need to disengage the YPL in order to check the system for suitable planets.

I checked my computers and could see that the system was within sub light drive access, the time had come for me to prepare for deceleration to sub light.

I climbed into my 'pod' and pressed the internal activation buttons which started the deceleration program, once the program had run and had been verified by my ship's main computer, the icy gases began to wash over me, 'this was my two hundredth sleep since my last landfall', I thought, and as I felt the chill rushing into my body, I wondered; 'Could this be the one?' in ten units I would be awake again, and would find out. Everything blacked out as I went as close to death as was possible without dying.

Under normal circumstances, some twenty units later, as I poured over the data scrolling across the screens in front of me, I would have discarded the system as I had so many others, the system records flashed the warning; 'UN-INHABITABLE UNDER ANY CIRCUMSTANCES' across the screen once the system's star had been identified, no other information was available.

I should have climbed back into my pod and without a moment's thought fired up the YPL and continued my searching. But for the first time in my life I was intrigued. For the first time in my life, I deviated from my strict regime of looking for perfection, and felt an urge to discover what the cryptic message meant.

It took fifty hours to reach the third planet of the eight planet system, time for me to evaluate the planet and decide if 'this was to be my home'. As I gazed at the vidiscreens checking the planet in minute detail, excitement began to fill my every fibre, 'How did they miss this little jewel?' I mused. The planet looked perfect, the land and sea stood out in stark contrast to each other, fluffy clouds hid the poles from my direct visuals, but the computer showed ice caps at both top and bottom of the planet, rejoicing in the beauty of the planet I followed the lines of the mountain range which stretched unbroken around the north pole.

My probes showed the northernmost of the two landmasses to be much larger than the forest covered equatorial, as I drew closer I could clearly make out gently undulating rivers flowing across vast open plains of purple grasslands which stretched for hundreds of klicks, from the mountains which ran in a ring around the planet, to the seashores at the equator. North of the first ring of mountains, the grassland savannah gave way to frozen snow covered desert, which continued all the way to the pole. Growing close to the equatorial seashores, were thick forests that covered the entire southern continent.

Both continents were in the top two thirds of the planet, one encompassed the North Pole and spread down the planet on all sides, covering almost half of it, the other not nearly as large, spread in a band around the planet south from the equator. The two land masses were in themselves great enough to have comfortably supported many millions of colonists, well the northern land mass was, the southern continent which stretched like a belt around the planet, as I looked again, was covered almost totally by a thick green forest, however a narrow black beach bordered the forests both north and south.

The northern land mass stretched no more than a few hundred klicks past the equator. The two continents were separated by a sea filled channel, of just over a hundred klicks wide separating the two land masses. There was a strip of water separating the two continents, the gap at its narrowest point, was no more than fifty klicks wide. The rest of the planet, the entire southern hemisphere was covered by water. The planet was encircled by an odd shaped moon, almost as though two moons were conjoined.

~

For my purposes the smaller continent was unsuitable so I concentrated on the larger, looking for a suitable spot for my new home, the belt of thick forest which surrounded the base of the continent stretched in the most part unbroken the entire way round the planet, but thinned to leave a wide beach of black sand and rocks almost a klick wide, the sea had a wide shallow drop off in the most part of almost half a klick, before it plunged to unfathomable depths just past a line of sharp rocks, which marched all around the planet and seemed to stand as a warning of the depths beyond.

I chose a part of the northern continent's southern shoreline, close to the narrowest part of the channel which divided the southern continent from the northern. At this point there were less outcrops of rock, to mess up my possible landing site, and ultimately my future home. Had there been no suitable landing point I would have ended my quest there and then. I would have moved on as I had done so many times in the past.

My choice was now down to one final decisive factor. I keyed the life support pod to bring Dominie and his beautiful Golden Queen back to join me. I valued Dominie's input, especially as he and his fellow Raybaros would be sharing the planet with me.

This time it all felt different, there was an abundance of water my probes told me, even the seas were not salty, purple topped grasses growing to a height of about forty centimetres and a variety of different types of trees and bushes. My computers registered no other life forms, the planet's soil and ecosystem would support the edible vegetables and fruits, seeds of which I had gathered from the many planets I had visited, all of them hardy and nutritious and able to grow and reproduce in almost all environments.

I began to log statistics; one complete revolution of the planet took just twenty point zero eight time units. The planet stood upright on its axis, with only a slight almost imperceptible wobble, that meant there would always be a uniform and unchanging climate in every part. My sensors showed the atmosphere to be gradually colder degree by degree as I aimed them further and further from the equator.

At the poles it was no more than twenty degrees below the freezing point of water, the winds that blew continuously at these latitudes although fierce, were almost gentle compared to some that I had experienced.

At the equator the temperature reached a balmy and constant thirty five degrees at its warmest.

The sun shone from a distance of one hundred and ninety two million klicks, and showed a red rim which indicated that it was aging, Checking against my computer-catalogue I found that it had been classified as one which stood a chance of going supernova, perhaps that had been the motive for the planet being discarded by the early settlers and tagged with the cryptic message.

Dominie, awake now stepped to my side and peered at the screen, 'WHAT YOU THINK JOE IS IT RIGHT FOR US?'

'I think so.'

According to all computer readouts the sun had more than nine hundred million years before it would explode, expanding outwards as a red giant and engulfing its planets in a massive ball of fire. before imploding to become a dwarf star, nine hundred million years might have seemed too short a time for the colonists, having millions of younger systems to choose from, fifty years was more than enough for me I thought, and I searched again to pinpoint a suitable landing site.

A stunted range of low rocky hills with snow dusted summits close to the equator boasted one truly outstanding peak, a dormant volcano some hundred and twenty klicks north of the ocean channel, this massive peak stood head and shoulders above the first mountain range, which marched clear around the globe some one hundred klicks further north, these two protrusions were the only breaks in the flat lands, which stood beyond the tree line. From the trees to another mountain range which encircled the North Pole. The grassland stretched from the strip of trees to the northern most mountain range, like a vast undulating purple topped ocean with the first circle of mountains and the single massive peak with its foothills being the only islands to be seen.

I noted a wide area some five hundred klicks long, and forty klicks wide to the south of the mid continental mountain range, which reminded me of a huge black scar, it was lacking vegetation of any kind.

On the next orbit I took a closer look at that barren region, it was as I had noticed without vegetation, nothing but dark sand and circular black rocky outcrops. If the sun had been much warmer it would have indeed been a most inhospitable place, but even so, no rivers crossed it, and it looked from my vantage point like a frozen black sea. It could have been the point of contact of a glancing meteor at some undeterminable occasion in the past. Here and there were other areas where trees grew, some sparsely, some as vast forests. Everywhere on the plains were outcrops of volcanic rock arranged in circles, almost like spears had been thrown from the heavens.

Closer to the North Pole, at least three thousand klicks away from the ocean, was another vast frozen mountain range which had first caught my eye, these massive peaks ran uninterrupted around the pole. At some long forgotten time substantial volcanic activity had poured out lava, building the mountains, whilst violent earthquakes had piled the land upon itself creating the foothills.

I chose my landing point carefully, planning ahead and considering my cargo, I had a weakness, I lived with twenty five pairs of the only Raybaros in existence, they lived in miniaturised state whilst in my presence, at full size just one of them would be too large to be on The Rambler. These cerebral creatures, the biggest, the reds, stood eye to eye with me. The Raybaros were as devoted to me as I was to them. Yes, I had shared my ship with fifty rare miniaturised Raybaros for almost twenty years.

I had visited a planet in secret, searching for my utopia, it had fit all my needs, apart from a few life forms that had shown on my sensors. I slipped down to the surface in my shuttle to check out the inconclusive readings. Once on the ground, I noticed that every creature on the planet was dead. I had heard of the phenomenon but had never experienced it before; someone told me it was a way of sterilizing a planet prior to colonisation. I had believed the happening was just a rumour, a spaceman's myth.

The first Raybaros I came across, almost the moment I landed, was a massive green, she was a beauty, in obvious distress, and she had flown straight to me as soon as she caught my thought pattern. She began broadcasting her anguish; she was lost, far from her eyrie, her natural navigation screwed up by whatever had destroyed all the other life forms. She was able to communicate with me through a form of telepathy, she could understand my speech, or at least the thoughts behind it, and I could understand the thoughts she sent to me. She miniaturised herself and I took her on board the shuttle. Shielded inside the metal walls her abilities returned. She directed me to her cave.

There was almost twenty of her kind in one cave, terrified and unable to leave. She told me of another cave with almost thirty others close by, who were in a similar situation. With her showing the way I collected them and with the twenty from her cave we left the planet, taking them to my ship. They have become my close and considerate companions, together we have conducted our search for a new planet, where we can live in peace.

Their speed and agility is remarkable to behold, I showed them at full size, hunting some six legged rodent like creatures. I kept and bred a few of the vicious nocturnal animals, primarily for display, with my hunting Raybaros.

As part of a show, when I made planet fall, I would give demonstrations of the speed and aerial agility of the Raybaros, exhibiting their skill at catching the shaggy six legged creatures. In most cases, it assisted in reducing the suspicions of a guarded colonist population, who having enjoyed the spectacle would then be more inclined to utilise my skills, in repairing their metal utensils, or be prepared to trade for new goods, replenishing my food and fuel stocks.

The Rambler was antiquated and not especially designed for atmospheric flight, under normal conditions I would have used my small shuttle to go planet side, but this time was different. I had no intention of leaving. This was now to be our home, and my computers had shown no life intelligent forms The air was good, the water drinkable, and the weather perfect, we were home and we were staying.

I knew I stood every chance of crash landing, but I took the ungainly, old space ship in just the same, initially we would need it to live in. I would have to 'belly down' as the 'skids' had long since been removed as being 'superfluous to requirements'. Choosing a stretch of beach that overlooked the strip of water separating the two continents, I aimed the unwieldy craft and began my descent towards the surface; I hoped that my chosen landing strip would not hold too many unseen rocky outcrops.

It could never have been called a text-book landing, the alucopper hull screamed in protest, as the old trading ship once more came into contact with and scraped along solid ground. Bucking and lurching across the beach the short stumpy wings, purely cosmetic once the ship was on the ground, were jettisoned to avoid snagging on any of the clumps of head high rocks or the ground, and flipping the ship over, causing even greater damage than I was prepared for.

Three huge parachutes unused for over five hundred years punched out of the back of the ship in a last minute effort to slow, within moments they had been torn away, leaving me to fight ineffectively with the controls, trusting more in fortune than my piloting ability, to keep the ship in one piece.

My luck had been running well up to that point, not only had I found my hermitage, but I had managed to keep the ship almost in one piece, the right way up and on the ground in almost a perfect position overlooking the inland strip of sea, some fifty metres from shore, the air was clear enough for me to make out the hazy outline of the distant southern continent.

I activated the resuscitation processes to revive the Raybaros and the ten massive rodents which took up a great deal of space in the hold, They were the size of a grizzly but longer in body to accommodate the extra set of legs, or so I was told. I had placed my Raybaros back into their cyro-cabs, freezing them to protect them during landing. I extracted all the pods with my seeds and plants. While the living creatures were reviving, unpacked them, into the air lock and remotely deposited them outside the ship.

Once the eaters were awake and active, I moved their cages, and placed them one by one in the airlock, and sent them out after the plants, I released them and watched through the visiview as they scampered, whimpering at being exposed to direct light, across the dark sand towards the shelter of various outcrops of rocks, where they immediately began to burrow, seeking the dark underground. 'They'll survive', I thought to myself, finding something to eat had never been a problem to them, for they would eat anything, and like all rodents they procreated prodigiously, reproducing a whole generation in less than sixty days, they would provide the Raybaros with sustenance for as long as I was alive, and for many centuries after if I was not mistaken.

I had been on the planet's surface for a little more than three hours before I had concluded all my tests and finally opened the outer air locks, allowing the crisp fresh air to flood the interior of the ship, and for me to take my first deep breath.

There was no need for me to be concerned about breathing the air as I knew from my tests that it was perfectly safe, the computers had shown that the atmosphere was harmless, even before I had made my decision to land, it was a little high in helium but I wasn't concerned about that, or the slight tightening it caused in my throat as I took that first breath, I could live with the unimportant irritation, for to me it was the sweetest breath I had ever drawn.

The sun had been climbing towards its peak when I decided to move outside my ship, I had brought out the Raybaros, using the remote lifting arm, actually I was surprised that it still worked when I exited the seeds and the eaters, but glad it did, it sped the process immensely. I arranged their pods in lines in the shade under the hull and left the resuscitation process to complete.

I felt quite warm and decided to strip off my alucloth suit, a part of my clothing that was generally never removed; the suit protected me, and all other space travellers, against accidental radiation leaks, which in the rust buckets that most of us flew, was a common occurrence.

I made my way naked to the nearby shore, rejoicing in the warm feel of the crisp black sand under my feet, and the heat of the sun on my back, I was in high spirits, my dreams had come true, I had found my planet, and because of the warning in the computa-catalogue, I could anticipate no visitors for the remainder of my life.

I had merely stepped to my waist into the water, when I noticed a flicker of movement out of the corner of my eye... I ran back to dry land to observe.

I looked into the water as I ran, and saw what looked like a shoal of huge black creatures, each about a metre tall, travelling just under the surface, coming directly at me.

I took a closer look from the shore; they were about three metres from me. The black creatures more like crustaceans than fish, with eight long legs, the front two with snapping pincers, a pendulous abdomen with a whip like tail; I presumed to be a sting. A stubby thorax, and a small head which appeared to be covered in eyes. A set of vicious looking mandibles, protruding from either side of an opening, that could only be a mouth. They reminded me of ancient vid pics that I had seen, a mixture of three primeval octopods, a lobster, a crab and a scorpion.

I sat down gingerly at the water's edge, irritated that any plans of swimming or even washing in the clear blue sea would have to be postponed for the near future, or at least until I could sort out some way of excluding the nasty looking beasts from where I wished to swim. I sat on the black sand, a little back from the water's edge, and considered my next move. I watched totally engrossed for a while, to see if any more of the creatures passed, and was pleased that none did.

Without warning I felt a sudden weakness coming over me, my joints began to cramp and my head started to swim with dizziness. I was enough of a deep spacer to recognise the symptoms, static electricity, crackling in the air, caused by a powerful and sustained burst of alpha-beta radiation. I stood and attempted to make my way back to my ship. I noticed the red halo which encircled the sun, had shifted in colour to deep green. Stumbling and staggering, half falling, each step seemed harder than the one which preceded it.

I now knew why potential colonists had discarded this planet.

The atmosphere seemed to thin as the sun reached its zenith, allowing the fatal rays, which felt as though they were boiling my blood, to come through with an even greater intensity, alpha-beta radiation beat down in waves, each burst of radiation intensifying the almost insufferable pain my already screaming neural responses were enduring.

Stumbling and falling flat on my face, I had almost reached my ship, having run and staggered for more than fifty meters, I rose to my knees gasping for air, pain washing over me repeatedly and without respite, I crawled the remaining few meters to reach the safety of the shadow under the ship's metal hull.

Unable to climb the short flight of steps, I turned to the line of cages which stood under the hull, the Raybaros seemed unaffected, my tormented mind screamed 'why me? – why now?' Through the pain I remembered the single rudimentary truth, alpha-beta radiation could only penetrate bare skin, the Raybaros were protected by their thick leathery hides.

I cursed the computer fault that had shown I was safe, and my own stupid impulse to strip off my protective alucloth suit and plunge naked into the sea.

The protection given by the steel hull gave me a moment's respite, and with my chest constricting in absolute agony, I knelt, gulping great breaths to give me strength. The radiation storm ended and the sun went back to normal, well if you call a sun with a red halo normal. I knew that my heart was giving out; it was struggling to pump the blood round my body. The pain crept to my shoulders, down my arms, my head was splitting, my teeth felt as though they were being dragged out of my head. Eventually the pain began to subside.

I turned to my beloved Raybaros, crawling on my hands and knees I opened the cyro-cabs one after the other, the uncomplicated task of pressing a button, sapped all of my remaining energy, until finally I could crawl no further. There were still four cabs left unopened, the remaining pairs who were still locked in looked at me quizzically through the glass view ports, as I fell forwards onto my face. Totally exhausted, powerless to move, my eyes were fixed open, unable to close of their own accord, I raised my head, half covered in clinging black sand. With an extreme effort I forced myself to my knees and crawled to the remaining cabs, opening each one seemed to take forever, but I persevered until I had finished.

As the last of the Raybaros, a pair of beautiful gold's, the smallest of my Raybaros companions, both of them nearly a meter in height, left their cage and walked across the black sand to join the others, who had been grouped around me quietly watching my actions, I fell back onto my face. I struggled to roll myself over onto my back, and with another supreme effort managed to lift my head and shoulders from the ground.

The alpha fall had lasted no longer than ten minutes, ten whole minutes to begin to die. My strength gave way again and I collapsed into the soft dark sand of my dream planet.

It was many hours later, I opened my eyes; the sky was littered with stars, with high clouds whipping across it. I lay for a moment or two, my body ached with pains that I had never imagined possible. My breathing laboured, I coughed and coughed, each time I did I brought up a mouthful of mucus. It felt as though my lungs were full of water and every cough was not clearing them but filling them.

I crawled up the ramp into my ship, getting to this desk with paper and pen has taken me the best part of two hours, a distance of less than 20 metres. I have decided to write this, rather than transcribe it into the computer records, for I spend more time coughing than I do speaking.

If I have managed to do nothing else in my life of any real worth, at least I hope to have completed this log before I die. I sense a need to warn anyone who follows me what this planet is and what it has done to me.

When I am feeling a better, for I know I should survive for at least a month, I am going to use my shuttle to seed different areas with my stocks of seeds and plants. Using the cyro-cabs which I will set to open at different times into the future, they will open and blast their contents over a five thousand meter radius. Why bother you ask? Well someone might have a need of them one day. I am going to move my shuttle closer to the mid continental mountain range, away from the equator and its Alpha-Beta fall, which will be a better home for my Raybaros; I hope that I will be successful.

I will set the seed pods at distances of two hundred klicks from each other, ten each in a Northerly, and also an Easterly direction, with a one hundred year increase in opening times for each pod. The last will open some two thousand years into the future.

The Raybaros are in agreement with me that there is sufficient fauna for their needs; having already flown, full sized, to the mountains and found a suitable habitation for their families. The snow capped peaks have a vast number of caves which would accommodate them easily.

I will attempt to move the shuttle in the morning.

~

This was the last entry in the log, which was presented to Q'asha by Lord Dominie of the M'ntar.

ONE THOUSAND SEVEN HUNDRED YEARS LATER

TYMOTH AND JONA

'Ready?' Jona's call came from outside the home-dome.

'Be rite' wit' ye!' Tymoth called back, and turned to his pledge Izzi.

'Gi's a huggie 'en,' she said, they embraced, he gave her a lingering kiss and a loving pat on her swollen belly, palmed the door pad and stepped outside.

'Alrite?'

'OK, yer?'

'Rockin''

'Good fushin' t'nite' Jona commented, as he and Tymoth stepped out together across the hard packed courtyard towards the beach.

'How's Izzi?' he continued without waiting for a reply, concern in his voice

'Aful close,' was Tymoth noncommittal reply.

As a rule such a personal question would be strictly taboo. But Jona was Izzi's twin sister Senna's pledge, as well as being Tymoth's closest friend. As such he had family rights, allowing him to inquire about personal matters.

'Q'asha up f'r it?' Jona asked as they walked to the boats.

'Aye,' Tymoth's grunt showed he was far from his usual garrulous self, and Jona backed off the subject and the questions.

As they walked, the huge cracked face of the ugly orange moon 'B'goi, with her piggy backing destroyer hanging malevolently over her shoulder, and her wispy red hair floating around her face, was beginning her journey into the sky, before covering almost the entire northern horizon. It would be an hour before the conjoined moons completed their climb. The sun had almost set in the west, the sky morphing to a rich deep purple after its recent conflagration of green and red.

'Rekon t'nicht 'll be a'rite' said Tymoth. He bent down to grab one of their 'yowies' handles. Jona took hold of the other handle, and after humping their fishing net into it, they carried the flat bottomed boat down to the shore, its associated ropes, the tows, slung in coils across their shoulders. They both held a long piko in their free hand.

Around them the five other pairs of fushmen on their shift were preparing their yowies, and as one they all waded into the inky black waters of the bay.

The little bay was the only safe haven along the known stretch of the shoreline.

'Ope Shenkies bide hame t'nite,' came a muttered comment from one of the nearest pair of fushmen, a powerfully built young woman.

'Aye,' Jona grunted.

They climbed into the fragile craft and pushed off. They were dressed warm to keep out the biting cold wind which blew onshore from dusk to dawn. Their fishing clothes, from their tammies, the knitted hats on their heads, down to the knee high, waterproof socks, their baffies, all many times re-knitted and resealed, were almost sufficient to keep out the wet and the numbing cold.

Eight generations had passed since the survivors of the underground Ark, affectionately known as Weegie City, had made their way to the surface. The enclosed encampment was surrounded on all sides by various creatures, most of them intent on making meals of us, the inhabitants. Of the original seven hundred and fifty thousand escapees who had disappeared into the depths of the earth, over four thousand six hundred and seventy years in the past, and of the three thousand Firster's, who had struggled out of the dying underground city, over one hundred and sixty years ago. Less than five hundred remain.

Their protective clothing and the yowies had been passed down through the generations from the Firster's, the original escapees from the depths of the under-world. The little boats had been built at least eight generations beforehand, from interwoven and glued strips of plastiwood. Salvaged from home-dome packing cases. The craft were roughly rectangular in shape, flat bottomed and flimsy, every generation had added to the many patches and repairs.

Taking an oar, shaped from a Radgie's shoulder blade each, and kneeling on the recently repaired hull, Tymoth and Jona swiftly and confidently pushed off into the gentle swell. It wasn't long before the shoreline had faded into the gloaming. Looking back they could still see the lights of the township dancing on the black sea. They pushed on, paddling out into the darkening bay.

B'goi had nearly filled the northern sky by the time they reached the reef; the sound of the surf stronger and louder as the tide advanced following the moon's pull, and approaching the fushin ledge. The dancing pale blue southern lights were beginning to fade from view.

~

It had taken roughly half an hour to reach the gap.

Water began lapping across the flat rocks, following the south to north pull of the moon as it lifted into the be-speckled sky. In response, all around the 'gap', waves began pounding on the sharp black rocks of the reef. By the time B'goi had reached its zenith, the noise of the crashing waves would be deafening.

As they waited for the gap to fill, one after another the yowies approached the shallow water, which had begun to flow across the flat bed of obsidian; the lead fushmen threw their nets into the deeper water at the far end of the slab. Together the teams sculled back to the 'quiet side'.

Holding fast to their tows, they waited for the Ouaouaron or Mas as they were commonly called, to run. The Mas would start their run, if they were going to, almost immediately B'goi had concluded its climb above the horizon, and had ended its pull of the surging, violent tidal waters towards the north.

A the moon climbed rapidly into the sky, the vast array of chakano, which had twinkled brightly between the clouds, began to fade as its sombre red light flooded the scene. The huge, angry, boiling clouds, which appeared on cue at nightfall, were once again rolling across the sky, driven by the bitterly cold winds which blew onshore from dusk until dawn. The clouds obscuring the moon's brilliance, as it sailed behind them, throwing huge shadows which galloped across the land.

Blue lights were flickering and dancing in the south, painting the southern sky with an eerie light all along and around the distant horizon, a pale blue which gradually faded as the huge moon approached and took control. But those lights would flow back into blue again once she had set. As Jona had predicted, everything seemed perfect for a good nights fishing.

The Mas would pass outside the 'gap', moving with the riptide to where less than a klick away, the River Soupan emptied into the sea. There so it was said, the Mas had once been observed following it inland, what they did then, no one knew. For generations, no one had been tempted to find out.

As they were 'running', the tide would every so often force Mas to come close to the gap. Sometimes close enough to be forced onto the black slab by the surging tide. There it would appear on the shelf. This was the moment the fushmen had been waiting for; skilfully they would pull the ropes, their tows, entangling the creature in their nets. The same cruive's, which the fushmen, and their pledges fastidiously repaired and maintained. Fishing for Mas was critical; in fact it was so crucial that the ongoing survival of the fort depended entirely upon it. The Mas were its most important food source; in fact they were almost its only food source.

THE MAS

'Hald tite they's runnin!' came the warning call from the far left of the arc, and the two young men, along with the other five pairs of their shift, readied themselves for the onslaught. The first Mas surfaced. The correct ropes were pulled, and it was quickly caught in a cruive. A boat surged forward, the lead fushman hauling on the rope and dragging the creature further in and across the gap. The Mas was like something out of a nightmare, standing half again the height of a full grown man, and more than three times as heavy.

Eight spindly legs which looked as though they would never be able to support its weight were scrabbling to free themselves from the cruive. It was attempting to bring its front legs, which were armed with vicious snapping pincers into play. Its tiny head which sported slashing mandibles snapped at the netting.

As the pair closed in on the hissing, screeching creature, one of the fushmen leaned out of the craft, as it reared up out of the shallow water attempting to attack them, stabbed it expertly in its under parts with his needle pointed piko. The creature gave a screech and collapsed, the two fushmen hauled it away from the swirling waters, back into the calmer township side of the gap. They quickly rowed through and towards the rear of the rough arc of boats, towing the dead nightmare with them. With a flick of their ropes the net opened.

Once released from the cruive the creature rolled over and floated on its back, a ghastly sight with its legs poking out in bizarre angles. It was surprisingly buoyant when dead. Swiftly the pair made their way back through their fellows, towards the violent end of the gap. Once there, they cast their cruive with a skill which belied their youth, plugging the space left open for them. They then rowed themselves back into the waiting semi-circle trailing their ropes; the whole episode had taken less than two minutes.

~

It was a hazardous occupation, fushin the Mas, for starters, getting to the point of managing to pierce their abdomens was another story. They were unpredictable and would attack, as easily as they would attempt to flee. A single puncture of their bloated pink abdomens was sufficient to kill them. No one understood why they died so easily, but the fushmen were thankful they did.

But Not so with the black Shenkies, - you knew where you were with the Shenkies, 'Deep in do-dos'. Although only half as big as the Mas when standing, they had an almost identical physical makeup, obviously a kindred species. But the Shenkies were tougher, more determined, and unlike the Mas obviously carnivores. They never considered flight an option.

The Shenkies sometimes took multiple piko thrusts, into their abdomens to kill. No piko stab however had managed to puncture either creature through its upper body carapace. However piercing either creature between their ring of eight eyes, caused them to perish immediately. But those eyes were protected behind vicious, curved mandibles. The latter technique was by far the dodgiest, but most effective way to kill them. Both creatures sported sharp snapping pincers on their front legs, which if they were able to grab and pierce a settler, could cut clean through his or her body, tearing the stomach open and gutting the luckless individual in moments. As an added extra to their already formidable arsenal of weapons, the Shenkies carried a whip like sting on a long tail, which almost always proved fatal.

It was without a doubt a much more horrific death to be caught by the killer Shenkies. For once caught in the razor sharp grip of a pair of pincers, the terrible black creature would then pull the luckless individual towards its head. The horrifying creature would split the luckless individual's flesh by rotating a circle of razor sharp teeth through his or her stomach wall. Then came the final horror; it would plunge its long proboscis into the still living, individual, and by sucking avidly, to the tune of horrific dying screams, drain whatever remained of life, along with their blood and other essential body fluids.

~

Jona was kneeling holding their cruive's ropes, Tymoth behind him on one knee with his paddle ready to push the little boat forward the moment a Mas stuck in their net. A shout came from close to the left hand side of the gap, where the closest boat was situated, 'Shenkies ahint!'

'Dam' 'eir eyes' muttered Jona, using his latest favourite saying, 'Now we's in far an affal boogerin.' At that moment their own ropes jerked as a Mas appeared on the shelf and stepped onto their net, Jona hauled skilfully on the tows, wrapping the cruive around the creature. Tymoth, mindful of the possibility that the killer Shenkies were close to the far end of the gap, thrust his paddle into the shallow water and stroked hard, the flimsy boat surged forward at his pull, his powerful strokes taking them to the calm edge of the gap within moments.

Tymoth dropped his paddle in the bottom of the boat and grabbed his piko waiting for his moment to strike. The Mas flailed, hissing and struggling in the net, without a clear shot Tymoth hesitated for a moment.

'Noo!' yelled Jona as the creature reared up. Without a moment's hesitation the sharpened piko was thrust out, at the last moment the creature twisted and the sharpened head scraped off the Mas' hard shell, the creature continued struggling, and slipped off the far edge, disappearing back into the deep roiling water. Jona wrapped the tows around his arm to secure them, and lifting their paddles the pair began a backwards pull, when suddenly the Mas was snatched by something.

'Shenkies got it, loose cruive! Open it up!' Tymoth yelled, grabbing his brother-in-law's belt and bracing his feet against the yowies' sides.

'Cannat tows' roond ma queets, I'll hae ta spike the booger, hald on!'

The rope was wrapped not only round Jona's arm, but had entangled his ankles. All slack in the line was disappearing fast as the Mas was drawn, complete with their net further away from the nearby edge of the gap. All of a sudden the ropes tightened, all slack gone. The Yowie lurched, now dragged in pursuit of the disappearing Mas.

The other fushmen were hard at work all around them, unable to assist. Each of the other five boats was occupied with entangled Mas in some way or other. As expected, the Mas had begun to panic, more and more of the creatures becoming caught in the nets. Confused by the presence of the killer Shenkies which were 'inanaboot' them they were running closer than ever to the gap in their attempts to escape.

The township had to be protected as well as fed. There could never be any thought of retreating; their loved ones were behind the thin line of 'kilties'; they would remain at their posts guarding the gap, until the last boat. To let the killer Shenkies or even the slightly more placid Mas pass, could spell a horrific death for anyone, or any of their animals which might happen to be outside the protection of a home-dome.

Jona and Tymoth knew from personal experience and the loss of a dear family member. They were fully aware how deadly even one of the Mas getting through their thin 'kiltie wall' could be, for over the years many of their colleagues had been killed or seriously maimed.

~

Jona lifted his piko, searching the foaming water ahead of them for any sign of the Shenkie which had stolen their catch, 'Dam eir eyes, this 'uns well grippy,' he shouted, and thrust his piko hard into the water at the violent edge of the gap the rope still fouled around his ankles, and Tymoth had momentarily released his hold on Jona's waist, whilst he pulled the slack ropes into the boat. He reached up and once again took hold of Jona's waist band, steadying his partner. Jona struck out again, this time hitting his target, he then swiftly thrust repeatedly at the same point, and all of a sudden the pull on the Mas was relaxed.

With the release of the pull, Jona fell back, landing almost on top of Tymoth. The boat rocked dangerously, but still continued its forward motion. They had by now almost reached the pounding waves, quick as a thought Jona let go of his piko and grabbed for his paddle. They had been dragged almost all the way to the end of the gap by the Shenkie, perilously close to the swirling spume outside the narrow opening. Both fully aware their flimsy, flat bottomed craft would capsize in moments if they were unable to stop their onward rush into the roiling waters of the riptide. Tymoth struggled out from under Jona, grabbed his paddle from the bottom of the boat and together they stroked hard, away from the danger, dragging the captured Mas, which was still struggling in their net, after them.

'Lost ma piko' shouted Jona.

'Better that 'n bein' chief guest at a pluntin'' Tymoth said in a hushed voice, shocked at how close they had been to disaster, and from his companion's quick backward glance, knew he had been heard.

'Aye, right there pal, still we got our Mas, 'n' a Shenkie too.'

Once they were back in calmer waters, Jona hefted Tymoth's piko and swiftly dispatched the struggling Mas. They towed it and the dead Shenkie, which was still clinging to the Mas' back, towards the rear of the semi-circle. Both quietly pondering 'what could have been' they set about releasing their catch. Initially they had to untangle the Shenkie from the net; they then added both creatures to the now increasing flotilla of grotesque bodies.

There was no time to waste thinking about what might have been, they were needed back at the gap. Quickly they resumed their position. The pair managed to net seven more Mas that run, without too much of a problem. Then as soon as it had begun, the 'run' was over. In the excitement two hours had passed. Changing colours in the southern sky pronounced the setting of B'goi, and before long the scene darkened as the dull red moonlight was replaced once more by the pale blue of the southern lights. The water level fell rapidly. The flat obsidian shelf of the gap once again exposed as the tide ebbed, falling back to many hundreds of paces off shore.

Linking their nets together, the fushmen rounded up the sixty five dead Mas, and paddling hard, towed them back towards the beach. Theirs was a twofold duty that had to be undertaken every night. For the Mas didn't always run as close to the gap, and had to be 'fished' whenever they did. The township had to be fed and protected from both the Mas and the Shenkies.

Exhausted after the half hour row to shore towing their haul, the teams beached their little boats, crunching through the recently fallen snow, which had laid a carpet of white across the black shingle. A cup of warm soup was passed to each of them and sipping on the warming beverage they made their ways home. The Mas that they had netted, and dragged ashore, were swiftly carried off to the prep-domes,

which were closest to the shore, by the waiting teams of kitchiedeems, the food preparers.
~

'A good kip' was about all any of them could think of, during which time the Mas would have been stripped of their exoskeletons, the bony shells which covered their backs' were retained, along with the legs, the pincers and the mandibles, to be carved or reshaped, creating a multitude of implements and ornaments. Every fushman and sodjer carried a razor sharp, curved sword fashioned from a Mas pincer. The pikos or spears they carried were created by fusing together Mas' leg segments.

The Shenkie proboscis and pincers were well prized, especially the proboscis which was a favourite amongst the musically gifted, who would fashion chanters, flutes and whistles from the rigid black tube. The black pincers were crafted into extremely sharp knives, carried only by those who could validate a Shenkie 'kill.

The Mas' lower abdomen skin was roasted to make a crisp, succulent crackling called Gratton, which was eaten at the traditional family evening meal. The remainder of the entire mass of sweet, edible flesh of the abdomen was cut into strips; most of which was hung in the drying domes, producing a tough dried meat which lasted for many a sevenday, providing sustenance for the township in times of lack.

This cured flesh known as pemic was permitted to be eaten at any time during the day, the remainder of fresh flesh would be distributed for the next two morning's meals, to be eaten as the sun rose, raw and fresh, breaking their religiously followed nine hour fast. Traditionally no food or drink was allowed after 'Oodooce', the clear water ceremony and prayer, until the sun rose the following morning, a hang-over from the times when food and drink was scarce and strictly rationed.

The inedible parts of the creature, mainly the head and the tiny thorax were thrown outside the high walls for the Radgies to dispose of as soon as the following night came. Fresh Mas flesh could be consumed raw without any ill effects, however the meat went bad quickly, and any over two days old was known as yavellers, which if eaten would cause a serious case of the squitters, which would last many days.

~

'S'later,' Tymoth shouted his to his brother-in-law and the other fushmen; it had been a good night, for this night no one had been injured or killed, and they had made a fine catch. A new piko for Jona, the only requirement.

~

He was looking forward to his three day break. Tonight's fishing meant the township had fresh morning food for a day or two. And the pemic stocks would be well replenished. However it could conceivably be some time before the unpredictable Mas ran close enough to the gap be fished. Or following some unpredictable internal command, they would run in vast numbers the following night. No matter what, the teams of Kiltie Fushmen, would have to be ready to fish the Mas and protect against Shenkies every night.

The township had to be fed, but more importantly protected; only the Kilties, stood each night between the horrifying creatures which could easily be swept up onto and across the narrow channel, making their way across the gap' giving them easy egress to our settlement, even though shifts of two Sodjers at a time, patrolled the shoreline each night and day.

~

Tymoth made his way wearily to his front door, sloshing through the now melting nege as the first rays of the sun began to light up the central courtyard. 'I's fair chuffin nakket,' he muttered under his breath as he palmed the entry pad.

165 YEARS BACK IN TIME

ANDRU'S STORY

After breakout from the depths of the earth, we spent the first night- in absolute trepidation expecting something to shatter the peaceful dark; each of us armed with anything we had, which could be used as a weapon.

I posted sentries all around.

A considerable number of us suffered vertigo for a few of days. The skies and surroundings were immense. After a few expeditions we chose a spot for our future home, with our backs to the sea.

We spent the first three weeks under canvas shelters with our animals, whilst we brought stocks and home-domes, from the stores at the Ark exit portal, pulled by horses on trailers, the two klicks to our chosen spot. We planned to erect around three hundred homes, two hundred with their backs creating an outer perimeter, with the remainder inside, creating two horseshoe shapes with their doorways facing inwards towards the waters of the bay.

For safety sake, and to stop them wandering off, we kept our beasts closely corralled each evening, sheltering them with us under canvas. It became what some might call 'serious foosty.'

We designated the first twenty structures, erected on both sides of the outer semicircle to be used as stables; they were closer to the bay. The sea water is clear and pure, surprisingly it is palatable. We have chosen however to pipe our water from a stream some one hundred or so yards away, running it through filters in each homedome, which we removed from the Ark stores. That way we can remove any unknown impurities, giving us pure water, 'oou dooce' as Max, my guard commander, called it.

We disposed of the waste from each dome, into a deep piped tunnel, dug on the opposite side of our settlement from the stream. It drained into the rough sea outside the bay.

There was a good sized field of tall grass between us and a wooded forest of tall trees; the closest of which was about two klicks or two thousand yards from our chosen area. The purple headed grass, which reached almost chest height, grew in profusion either side of our settlement. Our beasts after being fed on nothing but stale hay and mouldy grain for almost a year before our 'breakout' fell upon those plants hungrily. Some of the poor creatures had begun to look emaciated. It wasn't long before all of our beasts; horses, cattle and sheep were 'well stuck into' the grass. The 'hawgs' too were having a great time digging up the roots, and eating them with great relish.

I made a mental note to try the roots, if the pigs showed such enjoyment eating them; they might be worth checking out. When I did, I found them most astringent, but edible.

A river ran from the edge of the wooded area through distant fields to the seashore. It formed into a delta about three miles further along the shoreline. The nearby stream, we had chosen for our water supply, flowed from the wood in a bow shape. Its nearest point being from where we drew our water, it too then flowed towards the sea.

~

A strange phenomenon began, probably once a month, but without regularity, the sky would darken at around midday, the sun would be surrounded by a green ring. A radiation would fall from some strange source. It wouldn't happen every day but when it did it would cause severe blisters, and sometimes if sufficient skin was exposed, death from terrible burns. No one knew where it came from, but it seemed to coincide with the first appearance of the nocturnal Radgies. Each of us carried an aluminium cloak, which provided sufficient protection. No one moved anywhere without their oocloaks.

We called it 'The Fall.'

~

We began to let our beasts remain in the fields overnight, tended by a few herders who were happy to join them. I guess we had grown complacent...

~

'C'mon hon' she said taking hold of my hand.

'Far we off til?

'Naver you mind'

I let her lead me; Lisa my dog followed, we walked away from the others through the long grass towards the river. It was mid-morning, the air was still had 'a bittie a chill' in it but we were well wrappit up.

Lisa bounded ahead of us, every now and again leaping up to get her bearings, and probably to ensure we were following.

It had been four days since Richmond and I had returned the from the Exit Portal, in those four days a great deal of work had been completed, the outer ring of two hundred home domes was almost complete and the inner ring was taking shape as well.

~

I felt a little guilty leaving the work teams, but at Kathie's insistence that 'I take a wee break'; I had not too reluctantly followed her.

The walk was over far too quickly even though the point of the stream Kathie aimed for was about two of our klicks. As we approached we could see the beasts grazing the tops of the tall pink grasses. They were quickly beginning to put back the weight that they had lost, some were even getting a bit perky.

I noticed one of the bulls 'trying his luck' I looked away quick not wanting to seem interested, but Kathie had obviously noticed, for she took one look at me and gave my hand a quick squeeze.

'You next Dru?' she burst out laughing, I must a bin fair bursin, and coloured up even more, for she let go of my hand and laughing even louder, and dashed off after Lisa.

Spurred into action I ran after her, catching up within a few strides, I caught her around her waist and together we fell into a tangle of arms and legs. In moments we were clasped in the embrace that I had dreamt of since the moment I first clappit eyes on her.

'Calm down big'man' she said, 'Nae but a bittie more afore we c'n start playin yon games, you wantin yon lads n lassies to have a wide view of their elders cavortin' in the grass?'

I stood up reluctantly and hand in hand we carried on towards the river. It wasn't long before we reached the river bank and sat down on our alucloaks on the black sand, holding hands and enjoying the peace and quiet, the water flowed past gently, it was so clear we could see the bottom quite clearly. Lisa was lapping the crystal clear water like it was about to run out.

Kathie turned to me and once again our lips were drawn together, I felt myself falling into her wonderful green eyes. My imaginings had not been wrong, her body was perfect, she was slim with all the other pieces in the right places.

It was the first time for both of us, what started off as inexperienced fumbling soon sorted itself out as Mother Nature took over. We lay together afterwards enjoying the pleasure of the quiet, and each other's presence.

I felt a nudge on the side of my face, opening my eyes to see Lisa standing over me, she looked up at the sun, I followed her gaze, and then leapt up with a start.

'Get covered quickly!' I shouted.

We must have dozed off, the sun's corona was green, and edging towards dark green, another few moments and 'the fall' would begin. We threw our alu cloaks over our heads in time, I could see the colour of the sun in its reflection below us in the water, it was a horrifying sight, the entire sun turned a dark green for the ten frightening minutes that the phenomenon lasted.

I was almost sick as I thought of what could have happened to us if Lisa hadn't woken me. I will never know if she knew what she had done or if it was purely coincidence. I like to think she knew she had saved our lives.

When the fall was over, we walked quietly hand in hand along the river bank back towards the settlement's water pipe which we then followed back to the home-domes. We could see them from quite a distance off, glinting white in the early afternoon sunshine, looking for the entire world like a cluster of white balls which had been half buried in the sand.

As we reached the settlement we stopped to watch another dome inflating, as the outer skin grew to its full size we could hear the grounding spike driving down through the shingle to the bedrock below.

As the dome reached full size three young men quickly connected the input and waste water pipes which were then connected to the main pipes which had been buried in the ground all around the settlement, connecting in turn to the central hub.

'Goin' fine here Elder' shouted one of the lads, he was tall and dark skinned, like his fellows was stripped to the waist, with a crop of tangled white hair which reached down his tattooed shoulders almost to his shoulder blades.

'Hairs' called 'dreads'' Kathie said to me, almost as though she was reading my thoughts. I waved to the lad and was rewarded with the widest, whitest grin I had ever seen in my life.

'Rock on' I called out to them, using one of my newly learnt Rom expressions.

To which he and his colleagues punched their right fists in the air and in unison shouted back; 'Tommy.' They then burst out laughing and whistling.

'Did you see that strange happening with the sun,' I asked, wondering why they seemed so full of fun.

'No boss, nothing here,' said one, the others agreed.

'I guess that thing must be localised,' said Kathie.

Waving to them still intrigued, we walked away, through the other gangs of workers, all of them seemed happy and domes were going up like wildfire all around the two circles.

Three more grew out of their packing cases as we walked past.

~

'Not long before we can all start moving in,' said Richmond who had come up behind us as we paused for a moment on our tour.

'I guess that must be the outer circle almost done, time to get the remainder of the gear packed away before the morning snows ruin it,' I said to him.

'We're working on it already was his reply.

'Can't see why you need me,' I said feigning hurt.

'We gotta have someone to moan at' piped up Kathie.

'I guess' I said sulkily, the smile on my face giving lie to the whole interaction.

Kathie and I were still holding hands, I was almost afraid to let go in case I floated away, my happiness complete. Our close brush with death had faded into insignificance in the light of the worker's achievements; the little settlement was looking great.

'When you two gonna 'jump the broomstick'? Loads of kids are waiting for you two to lead the way,' said Max by way of greeting, never one to waste words was Max.

'As soon as the last dome is finished and we have all moved in,' I said.

Kathie looked sideways at me, 'Sorry, I was gonna ask you, but never had a chance,' I said lamely.

'Good job, then I might answer yes when you do decide to?'

Much to the delight of our colleagues we fell into another kiss.

It was a few nights later, in fact the night before the day we had chosen to 'jump the broomstick' we decided to join the herders out with the beasts, wrapping up against the cold, we set off with the night team, many of whom would be joining us in the wedding ceremony, it promised to be a real hoolie, a wild party.

VERSHENKO

I think we were being encouraged to spend the night away from the settlement so that preparations for the following day could be put in place, Kathie and I didn't really mind, it was an opportunity once again for us to be alone for a while.

After building a fire on the river bank, cutting down a pile of the older grasses, we had found that they burnt well and gave off a pleasant aroma, but rather a lot of smoke.

It was a great time, and Kathie and I were welcomed into the band of nearly fifteen couples, I noted that there were couples from both sides, and some who had crossed the divide and were about to join our groups together. I was pleased to note that our two groups are melding well.

We had brought with us in a tin, the remnants of the settlement's evening meal, it was some kind of stew, we had a real communal meal, all of us dipping into the huge chest high metal container, once it had been re-warmed over the fire, digging out chunks of meat and vegetables, the pieces were easily as large as both fists held together. The meal was delicious, warming, and was more than enough for all of us to eat our fill.

After the meal we sat around the fire, swapping stories of our lives, interspersed with singing lustily. The Roms loved singing and dancing, and taught us many songs and dance steps, it was a great time of getting to know each other. Kathie and I learned more about each other that night than we had in the whole time that we had been together. It was late when we decided to take to our bedrolls.

The sky which was full of stars was wonderful to behold, the constellations completely new to all of us. As we rolled into our blankets, Kathie and I lay for a while mesmerised by the absolute beauty of the heavenly display. Although our view was frequently obscured by the huge clouds which raced across the sky, pushed by high powerful winds, the view was almost overwhelming in its majesty.

Without a word we turned to each other and made love with such a tenderness that left both of us glowing with absolute satisfaction and whole love for each other.

The moon had by now fully risen, and was filling the sky in its mad rush to reach the northern horizon. Its passage was almost eerie as the landscape was painted red with huge moving black shadows cast by the racing clouds. We lay wrapped in each other's arms listening to the growing thunder of the distant waves, pounding on the shore line's rocks in response to the pull of the huge moon.

The tides pulled in and out twice a day, following the huge moon's passage around our new world. Our happiness seemed almost complete. Lisa, who was wrapped in a blanket at our feet began to snore gently, I reached out with a bare foot and gave her a little nudge.

'Ahm skunered' I said.

'Aye, me as well, let's try for a bittie a kip.'

'Later' I said and ran my hand down over her stomach reaching for her. She gave a little moan in the back of her throat, and arched towards me.

~

Two days after we had 'jumped the broomstick' it happened, our first disaster.

The one surviving youngster, out of the nine who were herding our beasts that night told a story of pure horror. The creatures had appeared at dawn proceeding from the vresh, the tree line, making their way towards the River.

Their destination it was assumed was the sea. They were doggedly following a route that the young herders had camped across with our livestock around them. The creatures made their way towards the river bank, directly towards our beasts.

Ringo, one of the Layfette, the only one who survived, once he could speak with any rationality told a story which chilled our blood.

'I was on the far side of the herd, when I heard a horrific screaming,' he said between sobs. 'It was coming on dawn and snowing gently. There was a damp mist all around me which restricted my view to but a few yards. I jumped up, and was about to follow the direction where the scream had come from, when out of the mist came horrors such as I have never known in my life, they stood at least head height and had eight legs, two of them armed with the most cruel pair of snapping pincers imaginable.'

'I ran sideways on to them, passing by them, I came across where three others fought against them. All eight died, I saw them fall, I tried to attack them from behind with a chunk of plastiwood, but they ignored me. And then I saw the other herders overcome and covered by the black monsters. There was nothing I could do, I had to run.'

The lad collapsed in tears.

~

Of our livestock there was not a sign of a single living creature. They had obviously run off, scattering in all directions away from the black horrors. Where they ended up we never discovered for no matter how much we searched we never found them.

Max and a group of his young bloods armed themselves, and swiftly ran to the spot Ringo had indicated to bring back our dead.

A large number of livestock lay where they too had been overcome, their bodies like those of our fallen friends shrunken and misshapen without body fluids.

Our eight fallen would be remembered for all times.

We named our settlement Fort Brimat in memory of one of the bravest fighters in that battle with the Vershenko, or Shenkies, as we came to call them. A young Rom lad called Brimmie who sadly lost his life, but not before Ringo saw him kill three of the creatures.

A NEW FOOD SOURCE

It was not long after the migration of the Shenkies that we encountered yet another variety of strange creature. Pink in colour, and identical in make-up to the Shenkies, but these stood twice as tall as the malevolent black killers, towering over us.

That they had the same nasty attitudes became markedly obvious the instant we came across them.

We discovered four of the nightmare creatures; they could only have come from the black waters of the bay, being incapable of climbing over the walls they had been trapped near our agri-fields.

They scuttled about on six long spindly legs waving two others in front of their heads which like the Shenkies were armed with the sharpest, most dangerous looking pincers. Each pincer was almost a yard in length, one snap of those huge blades could cause severe damage to man or beast.

Our dogs were first to attack, rushing around the bewildered horrors whilst we frantically hunted for any weapons to kill them.

'Ralphi, where's yon spikes left over from the wall buildin?'

'Ken em, Elder, they wiz by the beach homes.'

'Get you ower there quick, and bring em back we'll try'n hald the fekers here. Go! Shake it lad!'

Our dogs seemed sufficient to contain the creatures, their snapping and barking causing the horrors to spin in confusion, while attempting to catch the swiftly moving hounds with their snapping pincers.

The lad returned within moments with three stakes which had been left over from the wall fortifications, we made to face the horrors, would these huge creatures which stood taller than a grown man be difficult to kill, we were about to find out.

However the problem was taken out of our hands by one of the courageous dogs snarling like a bull Radgie he sped beneath the snapping pincers, and jumping high tore with his teeth at the creatures' abdomen. The monster immediately reared on its four hind legs, and with a hissing screech collapsed almost on top of the hound, which managed to skip out of the way in the nick of time.

Within a short while we dispatched the remaining three creatures without loss of life or limb I am pleased to report. However considering the difficulties our herders had battling the Shenkies, we were surprised at how easily these giant pink versions expired.

The hound which had dispatched the first creature, begun tearing away at the exposed under belly flesh, we watched in amazement as others joined it, obviously relishing the taste of the bloodless flesh.

Albie was the first to break from our watching circle. Running forward to the second creature he cut a piece of flesh from around the spear hole, without a thought to his own wellbeing popped it into his mouth.

'Watch yer sel Albie, yon could make yer serious ill!' I called. His beaming smile said it all; I cautiously tried one of the pieces which he passed me. We called others from their homes, and soon had a crowd around us, all keen to try the new taste.

Once we had tasted and approved we became a ravenous pack. We fell upon the creatures tearing off lumps of flesh, and stuffing our mouths full of the succulent pink flesh. To us who had been on a starvation diet since the Radgies appearance it was truly manna from heaven, well the sea anyway, the four creatures were enough to give us a meal, it was good to feel a satisfied stomach.

We couldn't wait for the next time the creatures would materialize; somehow we had to discover where they came from and how to catch them in sufficient numbers to provide us with a suitable and sustainable food source.

RADGIES

It was three months after the episode with the Shenkies that the next nightmare unfolded - we were discovered and overrun by the Radgies. They came after nightfall, snorting and snuffling around our homes, making prisoners of us from dusk to dawn. They returned the following night, and have ever since, howling and shrieking as they patrol, gaining access through some open spaces we had left between the homes.

Sleep was almost impossible in those early days; we took to snatching moments during the daylight hours. On the second night they broke through the temporary doors of our recently erected storage domes. Eating and spoiling almost everything we had carefully placed there. Any seeds we had were spoiled or eaten, spare clothing was ripped apart. Stored food was eaten, everything was fouled, the only foodstuffs that were salvageable in any real quantity were those in secure wooden crates, tins and sealed metal containers, some of which were difficult to open, some drums were almost half our height and it took two men to stretch their arms around them. Lifting one of them in a net cradle took six strong men.

One drum if strictly rationed provided enough food for up to fifty people. We began with about three hundred drums of various foodstuffs These had been in our initial haul of the rations, that we had 'liberated' from the cargo we found on break-out, obviously there to sustain us in the new world.

Opening the drums required us to cut off the restraining straps from the tops, for we had no other method available to us. The drums were filled with a diverse range of substances, providing us with an assortment of nutritious servings of food, but these meals would soon run out if we could not find a sustainable replacement.

Along with the food drums there were a number of large cans with indeterminable contents; these cans initially resisted all our attempts to open, but more on them later.

It was after the fifth sleepless night of horrendous noises that we decided that if we were to have any form of security, we would have to close the V shaped gaps between our outer circle of homes, for it was through these gaps that the six legged Radgies were clambering, gaining access to the areas between the inner circles.

Our plan was to fill the gaps with rocks, and sharpened stakes; we decided to bind the rocks together with the cement from the home erection kits; in that way we could build walls that were as impervious as our homes, and as high.

We used hoes, axes and shovels, which we had taken from the Ark, to build the walls, plasti-wood spikes made from empty crates protruded from the rocky walls creating what we hoped to be an impenetrable barrier. We shaped and sharpened those stakes with Mas pincers using the razor sharp inner edges. Those same pincers when carved, and shaped to fit our hands, made most useful knives and swords.

We hoped that the sharpened stakes would dissuade any Radgie climbers for the points were sharp, and we angled them downwards, with luck they would stab any climbing creature. When completed our settlements' outer walls seemed to be sufficiently difficult to climb for the Radgies' made no further attempts to break into our fortress.

FORT BRIMAT

Our settlement of white home-domes nestling close to the shoreline, if seen from the air would have given the impression of concentric circles of tightly placed white balls, half buried in the sand.

The outer perimeter of three hundred homes had been erected, each one touching at their bases. Inside the outer home-domes, one dome's distance inwards, was a further full circle of two hundred homes widely spaced, built two deep, back to back, with another inner circle of eighty domes which enclosed a large open area. Five hundred and eighty home-domes in all.

~

Each V shaped gap between the homes had been filled in with large stones which with the domes created an impenetrable wall surrounding the entire township. Apart from a narrow gateway which faced the north, the only other gap in the wall was facing the bay and that was thirty paces wide. The walls had been improved and strengthened by the addition of sharp outward facing stakes of plastiwood, the fill in walls were built to close up any spaces, between the self-inflating rock hard walls of the homes, and bonded with raw plasticrete from the Ark stores.

A casual observer would have expected the inhabitants of our township to be under siege. Under siege we truly were, for throughout the nine hours of darkness the many legged Radgies prowled outside our new walls. Their whistles, howls, hoots and grunts became as much a part of the night, as was our crazy huge moon.

The landward side of our township was ventured into after sunset only by the suicidal. We the inhabitants had intentionally cut ourselves off from the land, to give us protection from the nocturnal Radgies. Our ancestors had built high stone walls, continuing from the last of the home-domes, down the shingle beach to the sharp rocks of the bay. We could then at least feel that we had some measure of protection from the Radgies.

The Mas and the Shenkies could only gain access to the township by crossing the flat gap, the only opening in the sharp rocks of the reef. The Radgies had never been observed venturing into the sea; they too, seemed to be wary of the Shenkies that lived there. The only landward exit from the township was through a complex series of defended tunnels, turnstiles and twists that had been built into a deliberate opening in the wall. The opening was too tight and winding for the long bodied, Radgies to pass through without being trapped, and dispatched by the sodjers, our gate guards. The hideous creatures had long ago learnt not to bother. The designers had interspersed the passage with gates filled with sharp stakes of outward pointing plastiwood as a further precaution.

The pink Mas were rarely if ever observed out of water, but not so the black Shenkies which could be seen occasionally, roughly on a monthly basis during the early dawn, travelling in vast numbers, following the narrow stream bed. At its nearest point the stream passed a mere hundred, or so paces from our township walls. It was that same stream which supplied our water, through an underground piping system the Firster's had built.

The Shenkies would make their way through the early morning mist, the grimaca, as the sun was rising, after the Radgies had made their noisy exit, their path was towards the sea shore, they came from a distant tree line.

As a rule the vicious black creatures were single minded in their purpose, heading towards the sea in their thousands, making for where the stream met the estuary of the River Soupan, their only safe access to the sea. Usually they would take no notice of us or our homes. Knowing that violent aggressiveness was always displayed by the creatures, should an unwary settler or dog happen to be in their path. Constant alertness whilst the mist still hugged the ground had become our established way of life.

Once the mist had lifted, the Shenkies, and our other nemesis the Radgies, would have disappeared, the area outside the walls was ours again. The dogs could be let out and we could make any repairs to the 'burial circle' if required.

THE RAFT

We kept nightly watch on the shoreline for three days and nights before we understood the Mas, 'the food' as the Roms called them, came through a distant dap discernible only when the moon was high overhead. We could see it in the distance... a break in the sharp rocky reef that surrounded the bay. A break in the spray leaping above the natural harbour.

Richmond and I, with a brave crew of three others, took a hastily created raft across the bay to the gap. We were surprised at what we found, a gap measuring about ten yards wide by about thirty yards deep. The floor of the gap was a smooth black substance, almost like a slipway, unlike the sharp rocks which surrounded it and which fashioned the remainder of the reef. The rocks were formed of a hard black volcanic rock, the edges of which would easily slice the foot or hand of anyone unfortunate enough to slip and fall.

The gap looked almost machine made, how it had formed or been created was beyond our comprehension. 'Looks like it's been carved out' said Richmond,

'Aye, but by whom?' I responded.

'Let's hope we don't need to find out hey?'

Outside the reef the sea was wild, the tide rushing in and out in time with the daily revolutions of the moon. We named the moon B'goi after a legendary winged messenger the Rom taught us about. The sun we simply called 'The Sun'.

~

On our first night trip to the gap we saw them; it seemed they only moved at night, and then not every night. They followed the tide, each time it came in they would move with it, towards the north, we noticed Shenkies too, but they moved in the opposite direction to the Mas. When they met, the black creatures would viciously attack the pink ones, killing them impartially, the pinks would scatter, breaking their formation, and in what seemed like panic, swim closer to 'the gap', as we had named it.

Frequently one would appear on the slab, and occasionally if the tide was spate would make its way blindly towards the shallow end of the sloping rock face, there it would fall into the calm water. For a while it would swim aimlessly in circles before eventually making its way back across the gap into the raging sea beyond.

It took us four high tides for they only moved at high tide to complete our observations, and in that time using the raft, we had herded eight of the swimming monsters towards the shoreline, there they were swiftly dispatched by our fellows with sharpened spears.

We devised a method of fishing for the Mas which entailed us building boats from the planks of wood from the many crates in which our equipment had been packed. We broke open one of our few remaining tar drums, and coated the outsides of the boats with this noxious and toxic substance. However when it dried it was perfect, impervious to water and protection against the knocks and bumps the boats would be subjected to at the gap.

We built thirty boats, and using nets and ropes made from stripping lengths of alu-cloth strand by strand, and rubbing them together on our thighs, a trick learnt from the Rom women, created twine and ropes.

Creating the nets was initially hit and miss. We had to create them with sufficient strength to hold the Mas, but light enough to be thrown accurately enough to entangle a Mas, when it appeared on the shelf.

It took us more than four months to complete the preparation. On the first night's fishing the most able and toughest of our teams took to the boats, and made their way to the gap.

~

Our days were taken up with digging and creating the exterior barrier, and now our nights with fishing but at least we knew we were doing something to make survival possible.

Capturing the Mas was hit and miss at first. We lost a number of our 'fushmen' before a system was perfected, but even then many of our youngsters fell foul to the razor sharp pincers.

Initially, we used the raft to drag the dead Mas from the gap back to the shoreline where they were stripped and prepared.

It was a dark night some weeks later, the raft team were half way back out across the bay, having delivered a batch of eight Mas to the shore when the raft split apart, the team of seven were tipped into the inky black water, it took them over an hour to swim to shore. B'goi was about to sink below the horizon. Back at the gap the fishermen would be preparing to leave, and no doubt wondering where their support had disappeared to.

Two more boats with a large net made their way out to the gap but it would take them the best part of half an hour to reach the fushmen. The only way we now had of bringing the Mas to shore, was to tow them between the boats inside stretched nets.

THE EARLY YEARS

It took us six months working continuously in teams to complete the task of protecting our settlement. Two of the trailers from the Ark, strapped together, dragged by teams of ten, were used to transport sharp black rocks from along the shoreline; for we soon exhausted those in our surrounding area.

As a further deterrent we dug down into the shingle and using empty food drums full of rocks, filled a dyke almost 10 feet deep around the outer circle, our intention to dissuade the Radgies from tunnelling beneath the homes and walls, the dyke was a final undertaking which took us over a year to complete.

There were a substantial number of sacks of cement left over even after the homes were constructed. These had been intended to construct a complete town, we utilized them now.

We discovered whilst building our homes that the cement when mixed with the local black sand set like steel, and was impervious to almost anything including Radgies claws. We used our excess cement supplies to fortify the perimeter wall. Having erected as many homes as we could possibly foresee using, we felt that the cement was being utilized in a necessary way, and once we had completed the task the Radgies and Vershenko would not be capable of gaining access into our fortress with its fifteen foot high walls.

FISHING THE MAS

The sky was once again obscured by massive clouds marching towards the north blacking out the starlight. The teams made their way back to the shore keeping the flicking northern lights to their left, and when they came closer to shore the dim lights of Fort Brimat would guide them.

On their outward journey the northern lights would be to their right, even without the moon's light they knew the direction they were heading by the increasing sound of the waves, crashing up the beach towards the reef.

Initially we had two teams of towing men who were part of a fishing crew of eight boats, and would be interchanged with the Kilties as their turn came due. The gap fishers could be engaged for up to three hours or so whilst the Mas ran, during any quiet periods they would all spend their time preparing or repairing their nets and ropes, and resting before the next onslaught.

There were four teams of fishermen, each with a full team of reserves. Each team worked a full night before they were permitted three days rest prior to their next shift. The day following the exhausting shift was usually spent recovering from the arduous night's work, and the remainder of their rest period was taken up with net and wall maintenance with the occasional bout of Radgie hunting.

Joining a fishing team was the aim of every red blooded young man, they were the hunters, the providers, training was tough, skills at handling the skitterie boats, mastering the long spears which were used to kill the nightmare creatures, and building the strength of arm and back to last the long, dangerous and gruelling hours of the night took hard work and many months of training.

But as I said earlier dear reader there were queues of young men clamouring to join the teams even though the Mas pincers were capable of cutting a grown man in half, the word fear seemed to have disappeared from our vocabulary.

Our landward side held another problem which we had to deal with. We made weapons from the pincers, each fisherman 'fushman' and gate guard or 'sodjer' wore a curved sword fashioned from a Mas pincer. Our spears were made from Mas legs which although thin were incredibly strong. They were fused together using heat from our braziers; each spear required three leg segments to craft. The spears we called piko's after the Rom name, were sharpened to a point that was able to pierce anything, except the Mas' top carapace.

We practiced with our pikos until every man and woman in the fushing teams, and those hankering to join, could throw with amazing accuracy. We made targets of Mas heads aiming for the small gap between the circles of eyes, the weak spot.

Most of us could accomplish a killing strike from a distance of fifty paces or more. Missing could mean the difference between life and death, especially when facing the fearsome Shenkies.

~

We began to be blessed with children. Kathie and I had five; three boys and two girls. We named our children from the eldest; June, Josh, Ruben, Ruth and Marty, all names given in memory of family and friends underground in our former lives.

Our children were all born within the first twelve years of our arrival in Brimat, most of the other Firster's had children too, some of them even more than Kathie and I. The dogs too had multiplied, and our lives were filled with the sounds of delighted laughter and barking as they played together in the inner courtyard.

Were it not for the presence and hideous sounds of the Radgies each night, and the monthly reappearance of the Shenkies at our water acquisition site, combined with the irreplaceable loss of our livestock and most of our plants, we would have been content to carve our lives out of this rough and inhospitable land.

We had few plants left, some pieces of tattles, carrots and turnips were all we had managed to salvage from the mess the Radgie's had left, we carefully cultivated these pieces, some of them took and grew to plants.

We distributed the harvests amongst our population. The bobas grew, but were tough and fibrous, even after cutting them into small pieces they had to be boiled for a considerable while before they could be eaten. The potatoes disintegrated into a slimy mush, the turnips and carrots were tough and took a great deal of chewing. This seemed to no longer be a world for the ancient plants.

In addition we had to retain some of the harvest to replant, however without defined seasons, the plants grew throughout the year, a new seedling planted as soon as its predecessor had been dug up, helped with the quantities grown.

The work was tough, back breaking and requiring great stamina. Many of Max's people chose to be farmers or sodjers rather than fishermen, and their ability to wrest the bobas from the ground sustained us through the many times when the Mas failed to appear at the gap.

Needless to say they were necessary to provide some form of balanced diet for our people. It took almost all our daily lives, able-bodied young men and women to provide the food necessary to sustain us, working either in the veggie domes cutting up and preparing the tubers, or in the 'neep fields' at the top part of our settlement inside the inner ring of homes, where the plants were grown and harvested. The grass bulbs, once we became accustomed to them, provided another vegetable source, but one taken in small quantities.

Some of the homes in the outer ring had been given over to food preparation. Those closest to the shore to the dissection of the Mas, those around the neep fields to the arduous task of veggie preparation.

We discovered early on that Mas flesh if kept for longer than two days would go bad, once it had 'gone off' it would cause 'the Yavellers' a violent reaction resulting in vomiting and bowel ill health, high temperatures and severe skin eruptions like boils over the body. The illness usually lasted for at least six days but the after effects could linger for three times that until the individual was back to strength - some of our weaker members died from dehydration following a severe bout of the illness, even though we did everything to get fresh food and water into them.

FORTIFICATIONS

I originally thought that our time in this world would be short, that it would soon become too much for us. After the deaths of so many of our dear colleagues it would finally be the finish. What I had not counted on dear reader was the resourcefulness of the wonderful group of Firster's.

As you know from my previous entry, written all those years ago, we lost eight of our colleagues and all of our beasts in a horrifying battle with the Shenkies.

It was not until the following day when we were able once again to venture out of the comparative safety of our homes did we discover that all of our livestock had either been killed, or had run off towards the Vesh.

Along with the loss of two hundred head of cattle, one hundred horses, fifty pigs, and a flock of sheep, we lost four of our beloved dogs that fateful day.

NASWALERMO

Sadly dear reader I must now recount the most terrible time of all, Andru's writings pain me even now, even though over a century has passed since that horrendous time.

The Naswalemo came when the oldest of the Firster's children reached their thirtieth year, many of them had long since 'jumped the broomstick' and were parents in their own right, our numbers had been added to almost daily. The inner circles of home-domes were becoming quite crowded as family groups grew. Some of the braver couples had even taken up residence in the empty domes in the outer ring.

The Firster women had taught them the ways of birthing, and few deaths occurred during that exclusive 'women's time.' Their young daughters were easily as strong and as fierce as their brothers, joining the Mas fishing trips as full members of the teams, and making up numbers in the Radgie hunting parties, able to stand their own in either occupation. In fact almost as many women as men wore Radgie teeth sewn into the hoods of their oocloaks, their protective cloaks, as a mark of their kills.

Some of their grandchildren began to be born with an olive sheen to their skins no matter the colouring of their parents, in fact even if both parents were from the darker skinned Firster stock; their children were born blond haired, blue eyed and olive skinned. Disconcerting at first and a few accusations were levelled by unhappy dark skinned fathers, but as more and more children from all roots followed the same pattern, it was accepted that the planet's sun was responsible.

Q'ASHA'S NOTE: Even now, occasionally a dark haired and brown eyed child like me is born, but these became more and more the exception.

Their grandchildren were pretty much the same in stature, slim, wide shouldered boys and girls, unlike their Firster grandparents who were all sizes, mostly strong and tall reflecting their Rom and Weegie origins.

~

It came without warning, the eldest first born were the initial children to succumb, it was unlike anything they had any experience of. The opening signs were complete loss of energy, swiftly followed by a high fever. It was like an extreme form of the Yavellers. Within a day their skins had erupted into boils which quickly festered with the skin turning black all around the weeping wounds. They went down quickly from then on, and all without exception died by the fourth day. Not only was it the eldest that died, every one of the first born children from the eldest at thirty, to the youngest who was no more than ten. All suffered horribly, their parents could do nothing other than cool their fevers and pray to whoever was listening. I guess no one was, for they all passed away.

Their parent's grief was too much to bear, had it not been for their grandchildren, they would have been prepared to walk out into the night and give themselves to the Radgies. They had nowhere to bury the hundreds of dead children and young adults, so they built a circle of stones outside the walls and laid the bodies out for the Radgies to dispose of, it was the only way they could think of, had they buried them outside the walls their bodies would have been dug up by the scavenging creatures.

Radgie hunting was abandoned, a man nearing his sixties as our youngest Firster's were, was no match for a charging bull

Radgie. The night fishing was almost as hard to undertake, and for four years they lived hand to mouth, only catching and killing those Mas which managed to cross the gap and make their way across the bay, they were lucky if those numbered more than one or two a night.

They found a way around the Yavellers problem, one of the large tins remaining from the Underground storage provisions, contained salt, and another pepper, they developed a method of drying and curing the Mas flesh to create a crisp tough strip, they called it 'pemic', the curing allowed for the flesh to be eaten many weeks after processing. If the nightly catch was more than could be consumed within the two day period of safety, the balance was cut into strips and cured, providing them and down to us today, with emergency rations for the days when no Mas are caught.

Two of the home domes closest to the water's edge have been stripped of all furnishings and drying poles set up, with the heating units set to maximum they prove to be most effective at curing the Mas flesh.

It was when their eldest grandchildren reached sixteen years of age they decided, they the grandchildren, having been part of the shore hunters since the Naswalemo and having almost worn out the little boats by skimming around the bay and much to their grand-folks consternation frequently venturing to the gap, now insisted that they be allowed to resume Mas fishing. Initially after having shown amazing prowess with the nets and little boats, practicing daily on the beach between the two arms of home-domes, they developed a style quite different from that which the Firster's or even their parents had used. They restarted the night trips, initially once or twice a week.

Their success rate was good, sometimes even better than their parents or grandparents had ever achieved, the domes were soon full of excess meat drying to become the crisp dry 'pemic'.

TRUDIE

Andru you must take another wife,' said Kathie.

'Never!' Andru was adamant, 'I don't care how many of the other firsters have, but I won't, no matter how many arguments you bring up that the Naswalermo will never return, I'm not prepared to chance it.'

'But Dru, you know all of us Firster women were rendered infertile.'

'Then its up to our grandchildren to keep things going, not us!'

'You know that's not true, it's up to everybody who can have children to do what they can, you were party to the directive last month, and that directive includes all the 'Firster' men Dru, you especially. You must lead, you are our leader, we have to make sure that there are many children who can continue to keep the memories of Weegie alive, and it's our responsibility, our duty.'

When she was in one of these moods Andru knew he was in for a serious ear bashing he couldn't imagine being with anyone else, especially anyone as young as Trudi, the girl who Kathie had chosen to 'grow his seeds', he couldn't think of it as any other way. Trudi was our 'songbird' Charlie's granddaughter; she was sixteen years old.

'No way!' he said, knowing that he had lost.

~

His little Q'velen, Trudi's daughter, had been an absolute joy to him.

Her mother Trudi, and Kathie were the closest of friends. It was Trudi who helped him care for Kathie through that last year of her life, it was Trudi who was prepared to take the brunt of his rantings, his screaming at the injustice of the wasting sickness that dragged his darling Kathie from his arms. It is Trudi who has cared for him now that he too grows feeble, she has been a good wife, and although he cares deeply for her, he has never again been able to love the way he loved Kathie.

Kathie's passing those twelve long years ago, was almost too much for him to bear, but at least he has seen his great-grand children, and none of them, even though some of them have passed their thirtieth year, have shown signs of the Naswalemo.

Andru our first leader, one of the Firster's who came out of the Ark, has reached his eighty eighth year of life, and what a life it has been, his daughter, his grandchildren and his great-grandchildren know no other existence than this. He passed into the arms of his Kathie sixty five years after he led the Firster's from the deep hole.

FORT BRIMAT

Our bay has an all-encompassing black rocky reef, known by us as the 'Islands of B'goi, named after the craters and mountains which could be seen quite easily on the face of the moon. The line of needle sharp rocks gave ample protection to the natural inlet, the Mas and Shenkies could not cross them for fear of puncturing their abdomens. The Mas however were the only ones who came to the forest from the sea, but their route was further down the coast at the mouth of the Soupan river, they seemed to prefer to stay submerged.

The reef stood less than two klicks from our black shingle beach, separating our 'Bay of calm' from the 'Sea of death'. Outside the protection of the Islands of B'goi, the sea was a violent and dangerous place, tides ripping back and forth timed to B'goi's orbits. Rumour would have it that the rough sea was teeming with Mas and Shenkies.

The day began as it always did with a shower of snow before dawn; the sun seemed to struggle up from the horizon, fighting its way through the quickly dispersing mist, and promising the usual warm and bright day. The township began to wake; dogs were let out, and made their way through the gate to the outside fields, where they relieved themselves, digging shallow holes in the loose black chuckies, and then filling them in again with great enthusiasm.

Once they had finished their 'business', they would return to the township the way they exited, they spent some time in groups scampering around the centre courtyard, splashing through the swiftly melting snow, happy to be free after the long night's confines. It was not long though before they began returning to their owner's home-domes, tongues hanging out, panting happily and expectantly, looking for their morning meal.

The sounds of the night, the screams, the grunts and whistles of the Radgies were replaced by the excited barking of the rikonos, our dogs, the sounds of the Radgies faded as the huge, many legged nocturnal creatures sought the dark of their burrows, disappearing altogether before the first rays of the sun broke across the horizon, not to reappear again until the dark of the night had returned and was complete.

B'goi had had long departed from the clearing sky as the flickering blue northern lights faded at the coming of the brightening day, the fushmen had trudged home dejectedly from the beach, it had been a poor night's fushin only twenty Mas had appeared.

Every day was the same, predicting the weather was unnecessary, for there were no seasons, the planet stood upright on its axis, the climate was constant, the nights always cold, windy and cloudy, those clouds always discharging their snow showers timed perfectly with the end of B'goi's circuit of the planet, and by the time the sun had risen and the mist had burnt off, the day would be bright and warm, without a cloud to be seen.

As the sun rose higher in the sky, its red halo at dawn would sometimes change to an ominous green one which became an even darker green as midday approached, that was the warning to covrup, every settler had their own indestructible oocloak from birth, replaced as they grew older, which they either carried or wore throughout the day. The oocloaks or aluminium thread cloaks were a hand down from the final years underground, when tiny radiation leaks were detected around the nuclear power station which provided the city with its essential electrical needs.

At midday every one of us ensured that any exposed piece of skin on our bodies was covered for the short period of time, less than ten minutes, that we called 'The Fall', failure to follow this precaution was a sure and certain pathway to a painful and horrible death. It was a part of our daily lives, we were as used to it as we were to breathing, and 'covrin' was as important as that involuntary action. We knew not of the origin of the Fall, but of past experiences where others failed to cover-up.

There were four teams of fishermen, each with a full team of reserves, each team worked a full night before they were allowed three days rest prior to their next shift, the day following the exhausting shift was usually spent recovering from the arduous night's work, the remaining two days of their rest period was taken up with outer wall and cruive maintenance, and the thrill of Radgie hunting.

Getting into a fishing team was the aim of every red blooded young man and woman, they were the pinnacle, the providers, training was tough, skills at handling the skitterie boats, mastering the long spears which were used to kill the nightmare creatures, and building the strength of arm and back to last the long dangerous and gruelling hours through the night, took hard work and many months of training. But as I said earlier dear reader, there were queues of young people clamouring to join the teams, even though the Mas pincers were capable of cutting a grown man clean in half, fear seemed to have disappeared from our vocabulary.

Our landward side was another problem we had to deal with, we had made weapons from the pincers, each fisherman, and gate guard or sodjer wore a curved sword, fashioned from a Mas pincer, our spears were made from their legs, which although thin were incredibly strong, they were fused together using the heat from our cooking slabs, each piko required three leg segments to craft, the pikos, after the Rom name for spears, were sharpened to a point which was able to pierce anything except the Mas' or Shenkie's carapace.

We practiced with our pikos until every man and woman could throw one with amazing accuracy. We made targets from the

Mas heads, aiming for the small gap between the circle of eyes where we knew they and the Shenkies had a weak spot. Most of us could accomplish a killing strike from a distance of fifty paces or more. Missing could mean the difference between life and death, especially were we to ever face the fearsome Shenkies.

If it hadn't been for the presence and hideous sounds of the Radgies each and every night, that, and the irregular reappearance of the Shenkies marching over our water acquisition site, we would have been content to carve our lives out on this rough and inhospitable new version of our planet.

Many times we were forced to survive on the bulbous gourds, which we called boobas, dug from under the purple grasses, but they were not to our taste, the mush inside the gourds was bitter and consequently we only ate it in times of extreme lack.

Needless to say the boobas were necessary to provide some form of balanced diet for our people. It was part of daily lives for both men and women to provide the food necessary to sustain us, clothe us and craft the items for our daily lives. Everyone worked either fishing the Mas, or in the veggie domes cutting up and cooking the tubers. Almost the entire outer ring of domes had been given over to food preparation, by the kitchiedeems, those closest to the shore to the dissection and preparation of the Mas, those around the 'boobas' fields, to the arduous task of growing and cooking the tubers.

We discovered early on that Mas flesh, if kept for longer than two days would go bad. Once it had 'gone off' it would cause 'the Yavellers', a violent reaction, vomiting and diarrhoea, high temperatures, and severe skin eruptions like boils all over the body. The illness usually lasted for at least six days, but the after effects would linger for three times that length of time, until the individual was back to strength - some of our weaker and younger members died from dehydration following a severe bout of the illness, even though we did everything to get fresh food and water into them.

One night, almost three years after the elders had come to the settlement, ten of the wildest and toughest sodjers, armed to the teeth with Mas swords and pikos ventured out of the gates to try to capture one of the Radgies. We were intrigued to know what they were, for they bore no possible likeness to, what to us, were the indigenous creatures of this place, the Mas and the Shenkies. They stood chest height to a full grown man, with a multitude of legs and a body which was easily thirty foot in length. They could move at lightning speed and were deadly to say the least. The plan was to discover if they were edible, for we needed something to add to our now constant diet of Mas flesh and tough and tasteless veg. Immediately after B'goi made its appearance they left the gates, quickly formed up into a phalanx, with spears pointing outwards. It wasn't long before they came upon a pair of Radgies which were close to the wall, surrounding the formidable looking creatures was easy for the beasts showed no fear, Their leader Max, made the first kill, thrusting his piko down the throat of the charging creature, his lieutenant a huge bull of a man, dispatched the second as quickly.

The team, after tying ropes round the front legs of the first dead creature, proceeded to drag the heavy beast the fifty paces back to the gates. Within moments eight others drawn by the smell of blood came dashing up to claim the bodies. Others appeared out of the dark, approaching Max and his men with obvious menace. They showed no fear of the spears, they had never known resistance, and expected none. They were eating machines, and anything that existed was fair game.

Excited by the pungent smell of blood was enough to spur them into claiming their share of the bounty, a fierce fight broke out amongst the creatures as they jostled their way to be first to claim a share of the bounty. The men turned to face the charging beasts, their spears took down two more of the monsters, thankfully as one was killed those nearest would turn on their own dead and begin tearing lumps off the still twitching bodies, this gave the rear-guard Sodjers opportunitles they hadn't expected, the creatures were more interested in eating their own fallen than they were in attacking the small band of fierce humans.

The Sodjers scrambled through the gates closing the spike barriers behind them as they went. By the time the band had fought their way back in, there were at least fifty of the creatures, screeching and hooting as they ripped the bodies of their own fallen apart. It was to prove a fruitless exercise, for the meat was so tough and strong tasting that no one wanted to attempt more than a mouthful, even after it had been roasted for ages on our cook points, we tried boiling it but the taste was still more than most people however hungry, were prepared to stomach.

The hide however was a different thing, the skin was soft and pliable, and could be worked into wonderful soft leggings and jerkins, the bones when boiled gave us a useful glue which when dried was impervious to water, we used it to coat the outside of our clothes and knitted boots making them warm and snug, albeit a bit smelly, but we soon got used to it.

From the above you can gather that we made frequent forays, we made noose traps which we baited during the daylight hours with rancid Mas flesh, this way we caught many of the creatures, leaving them ensnared until daylight when their fellows sought the darkness of their burrows, closer to the distant tree line. They were dispatched in the daylight, providing us with a multitude of useful items and utensils, their bones, apart from the glue they provided, were tough and strong. But using our Mas and Shenkie pincer blades could be carved into smaller knife blades, needles and many other items. Their shoulder blades were easy to shape into paddles used nightly by our brave fushmen. The stylus I have used to write this journal is but one example; these items became so useful to us, that the crazy exercises required to obtain them, seemed well worth the effort.

Radgie teeth necklaces were prized by the girls and women, showing off the prowess of their men folk. A hunter who was prepared to risk life and limb to make a kill and claim the teeth, had prestige, for even though the creatures hated the sunlight, and would squint their eyes against it, almost blinded they were still a fearsome foe, even with a limb caught in a noose trap, they would fight until the last moment.

The dogs loved these hunting trips, and would tease the Radgies, running right up to them, barking and biting any of the legs, distracting the creature until the hunter could make his kill. More often than not a Radgie would break the restraining rope and charge at the hunters, dogs snapping and snarling all around the charging beast. It soon became a symbol of manhood to kill an attacking Radgie single handed, and the eye teeth were worn with pride. The teeth of a full grown bull Radgie were the most sought after. The fearsome creature stood as tall as a man and could cover the ground at a fantastic rate, matched only by our brave running dogs.

The preferred and most courageous, some would say crazy, method of killing them was to face the charging beast with a piko driven into the shingle and aimed at the snarling mouth. The impetus of the beast's charge would drive the piko into the creature's brain, killing it instantly. However a creature which easily weighed twenty times that of the human facing it, at full charge was not easily stopped. If the piko had not been placed exactly right or the hunter did not dive in the right direction, whichever could end in certain death.

Either way the young 'studs' had to learn quickly, or another pluntin, would be taking place. Thankfully not too many of our intrepid youngsters were killed, although some were injured quite horribly, and had to retire permanently from the sport. The practice continued for many years. Our children too were keen to prove their prowess when they came of age, but the sport came to conclusion suddenly, when the 'Naswalemo' brought everything to an end.

THE TWINS

There was no way anyone could have known that it was to be twins, I was the only person in the settlement with knowledge of anything medical, and I hadn't been able to deduce it. My short learning time had been crammed full of an extraordinary amount of teaching from my predecessor, the old, infirm, but wonderful First Keeper, Jen.

Two years before she died Jen had taught me to read. I then attempted to glean as much medical information I could, from the instructions on first aid, which she had found in the history 'strips.' However most of the directives spoke about medicinal equipment and drugs, which we did not have, or had ever even heard of, we ignored those bits.

I learned, as much as I could in that short period of time, about the secret women's time 'the naissance,' knowing that I was the only one who would be allowed to give any assistance to a prospective mother. When they arrived, the twin girls were named Izzi and Senna, they were my first call as a Sashfam, a midwife, they were my friend Sarii's first born, we were sixteen when they came.

They were beautiful, one dark haired and one brunette, in their colouring, both were unlike any child born for many a generation, other than myself of course. The Abiav, the celebration of birth ceremony, had been planned for months for one child. The celebration for the successful birth and the ceremony of naming which followed would normally have been over in an evening. This time though it went on for three whole days and nights. They were the first, and even up to this present day, the only set of twins to be born to us, for over one hundred and twenty five years.

They were of the seventh generation to be born on the Outside.

More extracts from my diaries

Q'ASHA

My teacher Jen came to mind. Jen had been the major force in shaping my life. Jen was already into her sixties when she was elected to be the first Keeper of the knowledge, she was the grand-chey, the granddaughter, of one of the 'Firster's,' those who had been in the settlement from the beginning, her purodat, had sat her on his knee and told her the funny, outrageous and sometimes creepy stories about the traditions and ways of his people, the Rom, she was taught all about the Smokies by her Gramma, secretly she preferred the Rom stories, but never let on.

Her Gramma was so tiny and frail that Jen found it hard to believe, she had survived everything that the Firster's, had had to face; some of their stories were horrifying, especially those which she told about the early years on Top.

Jen's father and mother were first generation, and were, along with all the other first born decimated by the Naswalemo. Since those days, whenever anyone died, the custom had been continued, the 'pluntin' would be carried out with prayer's to the Raybaros, blessings petitioned, and the body placed with veneration within the 'queir' the circle of stones.

~

When I was younger I remembered Jen had often been called on to tell the Darana Svatura, the secret stories, which she had learnt from her grandpa. In those days they still had disposable pieces of real wood and they would extravagantly build a fire in the middle of the central courtyard.

Once every sixday, there would be dog racing, footie games, storytelling, mouth music, singing, clapping and drumming and, even dancing. In those days there were still some stocks of the original rations left and even a little 'baurley-brae', the amber whiskey, which was strictly rationed and was only brought out at story times.

Following the final 'passing' of the 'Firster's', things began to change, our third generation ancestors began to revert to a more Weegie kind of attitude, a stricter more puritanical lifestyle was the norm by the time I was born. I am sixth generation, and a direct descendant of one of the Firster Travellers, with my dark hair which I insist on wearing long. The men folk tell me that I am good looking; I have dark brown eyes, and an olive skin.

I am tall, as tall as an Weegie male, and I know I have an fiery temper, which is often made manifest as I will tear a strip off anyone who fails to reach my high standards, I have never taken another pledge, there was only ever one man for me, his name was Paulo.

NAISSANCE

It was less than twenty minutes later when the girl opened her eyes, and with a start sat up and looked around herself, her eyes fell on the sleeping child and she relaxed, she seemed surprised to see me still sitting beside her bed.

'Peace chile', I said, 'ye slept well; yer man'll be hame soon, to see ye and yer first bornit'.

'I'd a crazy dream', said the girl, 'I be standin in a turn o' stones, and Raybaros be standin in a ring round me, and I wiz nae afeerd.'

'Wat they say?' I asked, I always become fully alert at any mention of the Raybaros.

'It wiz like t'be thoughts in ma head', she replied, 'Me minds wat they said', and as though she had learnt them by rote, she recited word for word in Engls, the old language, only usually spoken in formal occasions, and hardly ever in normal conversation, these words:

Your child will be a Traveller
A queen of far off lands
See wonders so fantastic
But she'll burn in the desert sands
Her perils and her triumphs
Will sound like wonders to your ears
But don't ever disbelieve them
For every one is true
Your daughter will be a great woman
And travel far off lands
And this girl child, young lady
Will bring riches to your hands

Q'REM

By the time she could walk, it was obvious that Q'rem was going to be different, not only was she brighter, more observant and quicker to learn than other children, her intelligence was that of a child more than twice her age. She tended to be a bit of a loner, preferring her own company to that of her noisy peers.

There were fewer children in the township these days, the once prolific settlers had stopped having children, not that they stopped trying, they stopped having. The rarity of a pregnancy and a successful naissance was always time for a wild party.

We still counted time in the old way, breaking the day into sixteen units, eight for the day and eight for the night, the method of counting the day's hours and the number of them, had been passed down from the 'Firster's' and although there had never been any clocks in the township, sundials had been built, which along with the position and colour of the sun in the sky gave us all a reasonably accurate indication of the time of day.

I could remember my own childhood less than thirty years before, when I was younger there had been many more children, but lately they had stopped coming, and along with the losses of fushmen to the Mas and the Shenkies, the home-domes were not as full as they once were, in fact hundreds of them were empty, stark reminders of the family names which had disappeared through lack of children, old age or misadventure.

I knew from 'the strips that when the bay had first been settled there had been many more people to accommodate, in some cases, there had been two families to a home-dome.

When she was about three years old, Q'rem started to have moments when she disappeared and no one was able to find her. Sometimes many hours later, she would suddenly reappear, surprised that once again she had been the cause of great concern to her mother; her aunt and myself.

She had been discovered at another time after a particularly long absence, a couple of years after her first disappearance, to everyone's horror, sitting on one of the highest points of the township walls, a fall from which would surely have been fatal, and where she hadn't been moments beforehand.

Q'rem had been gazing intently at a far off chain of mountains, in particular at the snow-capped peak of Ben Castra, the highest peak in the range. The range of mountains could easily be seen, reaching to the sky from above the line of flat topped trees known as 'the Vesh, just 'the Vesh'. Nothing else would do as a name, for that was what it was, 'the Vesh'.

No one in living memory who had ventured into 'the Vesh' had ever returned. It was voluntarily off limits, allegedly the spawning ground of the Shenkies.

The little girl had been oblivious to our calls, and even when a crowd had gathered and some of them started to climb up to attempt his rescue, she showed no fear and surprised us all by suddenly shinning down from the height of her own accord, she was five years old.

TI-TANTE SENNA

She spent a lot of time with her dark haired Ti-Tante Senna. Senna had always longed for children and doted on the little girl, treating her like her own, which secretly, she pretended to herself she was when they were together. Q'rem's mother Izzi, with some of the other young women, spent their day repairing the cruives or stripping and curing the Mas, work which took the whole of the day.

Senna would have loved to have been a part of that work force, to have been a part of the camaraderie and banter which flowed back and forth between the women, but an 'atraperdumal', a terrible accident had severed her right arm, a mute reminder of the tragic day when her uncle had been killed by a Mas that had managed to bypass the fushmen.

The nightmare creature had managed to cross the 'gap' unseen, and had made its way to the shore, its instincts driving it inland, it had not turned back to the sea but had waited confused, facing the point where it was stopped by the inside of the township wall. As dawn broke, once more following some inbuilt command or instinct, the Mas turned around and attempted to make its way back to the water.

The first person who blundered straight into it as she stepped out of her home-dome, was Senna, she was ten years old at the time, immediately it lashed out with one of its pincer bearing front legs, the snapping claws caught her by one arm as she turned to run, her screams had alerted others, and they ran to rescue her.

Her uncle, Paulo, her mother's older brother, and my one and only love, was first onto the scene, having beached his yowie. Devoid of any weapon other than his black Shenkie knife, he had launched himself without a thought for his own safety, at the gruesome creature, attempting to pierce its abdomen with a killing stroke.

As he ran towards it, it snapped at his body with its other front leg and managed to slice him open, clean through his lower abdomen with its slashing pincers, for a moment he hung in its grasp, then with a superhuman effort, twisting and pushing away from the grasping claws, he succeeded in ripping himself clear.

He staggered and almost fell his last step under the creature, his life blood, and what was left of his intestines spewing from the huge wound in his stomach, with a final extraordinary effort he managed to force his hand up and stab at its abdomen. He succeeded in piercing its fleshy under parts; the creature expired almost instantly, falling on him and crushing the last dying breath from his body.

Senna was released from the other pincer as the creature died, but her arm had been snapped, the muscles cut through, halfway between elbow and shoulder, blood poured from the wound. I removed what remained of her arm; then bound and sewed the stump before the girl bled to death. Senna never complained of the loss of her arm, in her own words she dismissed the injury saying 'Mashalla; me's lucky to be alive, no like ma poor noncy Paulo.'

Although she was a good wife to Jona, she regretted being unable to join the others at their work, and for something to do, had elected herself to be Q'rem's carer, allowing his mother to return to her indispensable position as a Kitchiedeem.

THE FALL

'Q'rem, where be ye?' she called again.

'Oh 'nfant ye'll be the death o me sure ye will' she muttered under her breath, Senna was desperate, she had been searching the township for the child for almost twenty minutes and had not seen a glimpse of her, aware that it was fast approaching 'the Fall' she began to panic.

'Q'rem! Ki!' she called again, almost freaking, where was she?

Would she remember that she had to 'covrup'? Senna's mind was in chaos.

She had only turned her back for a moment, and in that distracted moment, Q'rem had disappeared, in desperation Senna ran to the wall gate, she became aware of a strong impression that she should look outside the township, and so with a quick nod to the 'sodjers' she passed under the arch and through the turnstiles, threading her way through the maze of bends and gates, she came to the outside wall.

With her heart in her mouth she looked left and right trying to find him.

With a swallow to control her mounting distress, instinctively she began to follow the curving wall towards the north, hoping against hope that if she was outside, she was in the direction Senna felt compelled to follow, north towards the Vesh, rather than south towards the beach, the direction she would logically have chosen.

'Ki! Ki!' she called again and again, panic began to grip her as the sun's corona shifted to a darker green. Instinctively she pulled her oocloak hood up, and forced herself to run along the length of the wall.

Of a sudden she saw her, sat in the middle of the burial circle, something told her Q'rem was either asleep or in a trance; her little oocloak had been dropped outside the circle. Within moments the fall was due to begin, she screamed her name again and running as fast as she could across the loose shingle, oblivious of the fact that her own hood had slipped back onto her shoulders, she stumbled to the circle, grabbed Q'rem's oocloak and almost launching herself across the divide threw it over her head and body.

She felt a painful stab on her exposed skin, it was the final warning. With a scream at the little girl to keep still, she pulled her own hood over her head and covrin herself, flopped down beside her, whipping her exposed ankles out of the sun's lethal rays.

Ensuring the lass's little body was fully covered she held her tight, waiting impatiently for the fall to end, then picking the girl up with her one arm she 'hoiked' her onto her hip and walked quickly back to the gate, all the while Q'rem had not stirred, she seemed to be in the same stupor as when Senna had found her.

'Oh Q'rem, m'lassie, fy'de ye de 'is?' She scolded the little girl, 'Why lass, oh why?' Her heart still hadn't stopped pounding as she made her way back through the gate and once inside the township, she put the child on the ground, sat down beside her and began to sob uncontrollably.

'Ti-Tante, for what you cryin? Q'rem's little voice was concerned, worried, and at the same time strangely detached, seeming to come from inside her head, Senna opened her eyes and saw that she was standing right in front of her, Q'rem's head level with hers. 'Don't cry Tante,' with a shock Senna realised that the child hadn't moved her lips, she raised her arm beckoning, 'Gies a huggie en', the little girl moved forward to her, Senna's arm went tightly round her hugging her close. 'Dinnat run off agin' chile, me's a right feartie-coo. I mi'nae find yer next time'

'Oh Ti-Tante' she said aloud this time, 'me's fine, I be a talking to 'em, ay wodne le me be crank, ay tol me so'

Perplexed, Q'rem's aunt stood up took her hand, and they walked together back to her home-dome. 'Come 'n ha' ee a wee drinkie, ee mus' ha' a terrible thirst,' she said, 'Me knows I ha', I wiz well feart,' she added, 'Tis a guid thing yer mammy didne find ye, yed a had a richt boogerin.' Together they walked, her hand grasping Q'rem's firmly; to a casual onlooker it would have been difficult, to work out who was leading who.

~

It was later in the day when Izzi and I came to collect Q'rem that Senna plucked up the courage to tell her sister about the child's latest disappearance, and to mention the strange phenomenon of her talking so clearly, without moving her lips. Izzi was horrified to hear of the episode at the circle, and I'm sure I too began to feel doubts in her sister's ability to cope with the unpredictable, growing youngster.

At that point Q'rem looked up from the plastiwood toy she was putting together, looking straight at his mother she said firmly; 'But twern't T-Tante's fault ma, I be a talkin t'em, 'n ee say me be fine, nae t'worry bout onythin. But t'wonnie happen again, 'ey promises.'

Izzi was taken aback at this, for her concern had been in her mind, how could the child have known what she was thinking, and who she wondered desperately had Q'rem been talking to.

I gently touched Izzi's elbow at this point, 'talk t' ye later hon' I said, 'I'll mak' it all clear to ye when ye's at hame, t'nite wi yer man.' I turned on my heel, palmed the door release and stepped outside almost before the door had hissed fully open.

It was later that afternoon, before sunset, that I called at Tymoth and Izzi's home-dome. 'Come in 'Keeper'' Tymoth said, answering the door to me, and in deference to my position giving me my rightful title.

I nodded in response, and replied in kind. 'Fushman, I bids you clear nights and safe catchings.'

He stepped back and allowed me access. The room was gently lit, the little family were sat at the table awaiting my arrival, before eating their evening portions of roasted Mas flesh, and the tiny smattering of chewy root vegetables that they had been allocated.

'Te avel angla tute, kodo khabe tai kado pimo tai menge pe sastimaste,' Tymoth intoned in the formal sing song; guest to meal, welcoming prayer.

'Stanki nashti chi arankpe manushen shai,' I replied in the same ritualistic manner, accepting the meal and water which would follow; I took the stool he offered.

Izzi moved quickly to the warmer, extracted another portion of food, and placed it in front of me, in silence we each acknowledged the Raybaros for our continued existence and with our carved bone fourshettes picked up strips of the steaming crispy pink flesh, and began to eat.

After our silent meal, we stood and drank the oodooce, the fresh water from the home-dome filter, and reverently intoned the ritual words 'Me piav pani' as we drained the last drop in our carved mugs. This completed the meal, and we were released from the strict formal procedure of the eating ceremony, to speak.

I waited until the little girl had been dispatched upstairs to bed, then sitting down with the young man and his pledge in the seating room, I began my story.

'Many years ago I was called to be 'Keeper', not for any other reason but that 'Keeper Jen' who was keeper before me, had heard me say that I could hear voices in my head when I was a child. As I grew older, passing my twelfth year, I began to be able to hear them more and more, they weren't voices from people, but the voices I heard were those of the 'Raybaros',' as these were facts that the young couple were already aware of, they nodded in understanding.

'I think that Q'rem is to be the next, 'Keeper'' I continued, Izzi's eyes opened wide, 'In fact I think that she will be a great 'Keeper,' for I was into my early teens before I could hear or speak to the Raybaros as she already seems to be able to do, one thing more that she has demonstrated today is to speak to and hear other people, like his Aunt, with his mind, I have never been able to even hear what other people are thinking, although I have in a small way sometimes been able to make people do what I want them to.'

'Can you really hear the Great Ones too, Lady Q'asha' came a voice in my head, and I realised with a start that the little girl had been 'listening' to my thoughts all the time I had been speaking,

'Yes child, I can' I replied, attempting to speak for the first time with my mind to another human, I was utterly shocked that she could hear and speak to me, 'How long have you been able to hear and speak thoughts?' I continued.

'Just properly from today' she replied. 'you know I have been able to hear them, and to sometimes speak to them for a long time, but today they showed me how to hear and to talk to people too' she then continued in a more excited manner, 'today they let me see their mountain home through their eyes, it is so beautiful, but so cold, much colder than here'.

Her intonation was so clear and precise that it was hard for me to believe that it came from a six year old child, her articulation and command of language was more that of a learned adult. I deliberated for a moment and then realised that which she was achieving, that which I perceived to be words in pure Engls, without accent or dialect, were in fact thoughts which originated in her mind, and which then became understandable words, as clear as spoken speech, interpreted by my own mind into words I could hear inside my head.

~

Her parents unaware of the interchange, had sat waiting expectantly while I sat conversing in silence, they were perplexed at the shock which was showing quite plainly in my face. At last I broke the silence; I shook my head and blinked my eyes as though I was bringing my head out of a bucket of water.

'Q'rem must start her learning now,' I said aloud in a voice that brooked no objections, 'She is to be my apprentice, starting in the morning'

The young couple looked at each other, and with something akin to alarm in their eyes, nodded their agreement.

SHENKIES

It was one night when the cloud cover was particularly heavy, the Shenkies were seen amongst the Mas in vast numbers, normally Shenkies amongst the Mas would have been the signal that a good harvest was due, as they would herd their pink cousins towards the gap. But this night the Shenkies were in greater numbers than we had ever seen before, scores of them were tearing into the Mas.

They could be seen climbing onto the pink creatures, piercing them behind their heads with their proboscises, we could only assume that they were feeding on the Mas, for they had employed the same attack method upon us. The Mas in their turn were hissing in fear, many of them climbing on to the gap slipway in an effort to escape, some of those which had been caught by the Shenkies, appeared with the black monsters still riding them. Using the nets became arbitrary as the numbers were too great to fish. We could do no more than attempt to ensure that none passed our thin line.

The Mas scrambled across the gap to the shallow waters on our side, facing them were six boats with our youngsters two to a boat, armed with nothing more than nets, shivs and pikos.

'Hald fast team, keep yer pikos up, face the feckers, we cannat let ony through' came a call from the lead boat. Nikki's young partner Gorg knelt in the back of the tiny yowie, his face set, watching for any Mas escaping towards the shallow side of the gap, his shoulders wide and strong, his paddle lovingly crafted from a bull Radgie shoulder blade, was ready to dip into the water and haul them towards any threat.

'Let's go!' he shouted and his blade dug the water, the yowie shot forward in response to his powerful stroke. Nikki readied herself for the confrontation, her eyes fixed not on the Mas which was thrashing about in its death throes, but on the black shape riding high, clinging to its back.

'Gonna bag me that Shenk!' she yelled, 'Bring us closer Gorg.'

'Dinna lose yon piko though,' he replied, as he spun the tiny craft closer and broadside on to the struggling pair of monsters.

'As if?' was her reply as she threw the piko with unerring accuracy at the Shenkie's head, it pierced the ring of eyes almost at the perfect centre, killing the beast instantly, the Mas, dead was no longer a threat.

Hauling on the thin return rope, she pulled the piko back and within moments was ready for their next adversary. As they turned the boat back towards the gap, they were horrified to see one of their sister craft about to be overcome by six Shenkies, the two man crew were fighting hand to hand with their Shenkie knives hacking and thrusting at the black monsters which were crawling up over the side of the boat.

Gorg spun the yowie again and dug his blade in deep, sending them rushing towards the luckless pair. Nikki lifted her piko, she had one opportunity and took it, the piko flashed across the distance of twenty paces, piercing one of the Shenkies clean through its abdomen, she pulled the piko clear and dragged it back through the water back to her.

'Fek, its still alive' she shouted, 'Im needin another shottie'.

'We's too late' said Gorg, and they watched horrified as more Shenkies swarmed over the pair, their screams haunted her nightmares for many years. In desperation she tried again to piko the black creature, this time managing to pierce one between its circle of eyes. She felt no exhilaration at the kill, all she wanted was to avenge the pair of Fushmen and to protect against any other monsters getting past them. The boat was bobbing empty, carried by the undertow currents out to sea, of the two fushmen there was no sign, they had disappeared into the deep pounding waters at the end of the gap, both of them covered by the black horrors.

Almost immediately they had to face Shenkies again, this time three of the black creatures came towards them across the gap, Gorg threw his paddle into the bottom of the boat and lifted his piko, 'We got one chance,' he said, 'Tak th'one your side, I'll do mine, then ifn we's still here, we both go for yon big fecker in the middle.'

She grunted in response and lifted her piko to the throwing position.

'Nae lass, we gonna ha to spike the bastads!'

The creatures were less than a few arms lengths from them, Gorg thrust out with his piko, catching the creature on his side with a clean killing stab, he spun towards the centre creature, but it was too close for him to stab, Nikki too, had managed to swiftly despatch the creature on her side, and spun to face the second monster, she too, was too close to be able to pull back her piko for another stab.

Without a second thought she had dropped her piko and drew her short stabbing knife, carved from a Radgie leg bone, inherited from her father. With a cry of desperation, or was it battle lust, she threw herself out of the boat at the Shenkie, amazingly she landed directly in front of it, the water coming up to her knees. Before the Shenkie could register her sudden arrival, its focus having been on Gorg, and swing its pincers to attack, she stabbed it within its circle of eyes. Gorg, who had been moments away from being assailed by the creature, fell back on his rump in the boat, with a loud explosion of breath.

She climbed into the bobbing craft in front of him. 'Row buds,' she shouted, 'we's still got work to do! Didja think I wis gonna let a Shenkie tak ma Pledge?'

Over the next few weeks the attacks by the Shenkies became more and more frequent, and for a while they were fought almost three out of five moon rises, for the most part the young 'Fushmen' spent their time protecting the settlement from attack, they were able to make enough kills of the Mas to keep us provided with rations. Then as suddenly as they began, the Shenkie attacks diminished, it was then rare to glimpse them amongst the Mas herds.

SEVEN YEARS LATER.

Extracts from Q'rem's (Pronounced Kirem) journal.

TYBOT

'C'mon ma precious!' I said muttering the words under my breath.

Even though the pup had lost sight of me I knew from his mind shape exactly where he was. I could taste the air the young pup was sniffing. The little 'chaser' hadn't been following closely enough for me, I wanted him close by for Shenkies had marched earlier.

'Keep up lad' I called in a loud voice, the pup responded by dropping his head, casting about for my scent. Instinctively he began to move in a wide circle nose to the ground searching. Once he had me he lifted his head and with a joyful yelp broke into a long legged, ungainly caricature of the powerful gallop that one day would typify what he had been born for; running and running fast.

~

This is how we came to be together, from the day we met we have been joined; companions forever.

~

'It's your fete day lass' said Q'asha, 'your folks and me 'greed it be time for you to bond so let's see if'n we can link ye wi a rikono.'

I was twelve years old; I remember the excitement as though it were yesterday. I had been under Q'asha's tutorage for over six years and during that time I think she had begun to wonder who was teaching who. I know she considered that she had benefited as much as I had.

They tell me that I'm tall for my age, like most other girls I have blonde hair, with dark olive skin and blue eyes. Hopefully one day I will be like my father powerfully built, but as yet I still mirror my mother's looks and slim stature.

I have been 'opened' for six years. Six years since the Raybaros changed my life forever. Although I had not been able to 'speak' directly with Q'asha in the beginning, from the moment they opened my mind I could, at any time and from any distance. She however can only 'hear' me when I allow it.

Q'asha has documented my early years in a journal; I feel therefore it is unnecessary for me to go through them again, for her memories of that time are usually better than mine.

There have been occasions during the early years when I wished I didn't read minds, for I learned the hard way how to 'switch off' thoughts. Filtering them out until all I can perceive is a low hum in the background. I have always tried to allow others their privacy.

In the early days when I was a small child - even though the Raybaros had shown me how to 'select' thoughts, it was difficult and painful to attempt to block out all the minds which seemed to swim around me, hammering at my 'inside ears' as I called them.

Not once but many times had Q'asha or my Ti-Tante had found me curled in a ball my hands over my ears or hiding in some dark corner of the township crying with pain and confusion, trying to block out the cacophony of voices and emotions rampaging through my head.

But this day I was bubbling with excitement, as we drew near my nonko, Jona's home. I knew that Caspa had produced a litter. Convention did not allow any human other than the mother rikono's companion to have contact with, or even see the pups before they were ready to bond. I knew that it would be the pup that would choose me and not the other way round, for the bonding would be for the rikono's entire life.

In the past there had been many occasions when there had not been a connection, and a prospective human companion would have to wait until the next litter was ready to bond, before or even if, he or she would be chosen. There was no refuting the depth of love the two would have for each other from the bonding instant onwards. But it was the young rikono that made the choice, not the human partner. From the moment of bonding each would lay down their lives for the other; it was a mutual companionship, not a master and pet arrangement.

Caspa had littered four pups; they had been uncontrollable since dawn. The pups knew today would be the day of their bonding and they were as excited as their prospective human partners.

Apart from myself there were five other youngsters who had been chosen by the elders and put forward for bonding.

I was the youngest by at least two years but the others knew me for my position as Q'asha's apprentice and none offered any objection, even though numbers determined that two would be unsuccessful that day.

~

I rapped on the entry block outside Jona's home. Once inside, we six were led by my Ti-Tante Senna, making our way in a single file through to an out-of-the-way, quiet room behind the food prep area. I had been in the home many times but had never seen this secret room.

Caspa sat at Jona's feet watching closely, anxiously awaiting the outcome of the proceedings. The four pups lay quietly in front of her their eyes shining with excitement as us six; four boys and two girls entered the room.

The other youngsters and I were stood along a wall with our backs to it and as instructed by Senna, we stood an arms distance apart.

For what seemed like forever we waited with our eyes closed. I shut my mind aware of the seriousness of the moment; I didn't want to influence anything, which I could easily have done. There was a gasp from beside me as a puppy chose its lifelong companion scampering forward and licking the feet of a boy who immediately sat on the floor and drew the young rikono onto his lap. This happened twice more I knew now that only one pup remained and my heart began to sink as I imagined having to wait 'till another litter was ready for bonding, and worst of all; having been refused once would I ever be selected again?

I felt a cold nose touch my knee followed by a warm and wet tongue which licked my bare feet. My heart leapt with joy without thinking I reached out with my mind to join with the pup. There was a moment of a warm mushy sensation, and then as I connected properly I felt an overwhelming rush of love emanating from the little rikono. Immediately I responded in like manner, and slid down the wall gathering him into my arms. I felt so complete as the little pure white pup and I became one in our mutual acceptance of each other.

'Ee be Tybot' I said aloud and named the pup. He responded to my words with the delivery of a full face wash, which brought a gale of laughter from my Uncle, yelps of delight and cheers from the others in the room, followed by a further face wash from the pup.

'It's been a richt fine bonding' said Jona. Caspa's tail confirmed her agreement.

Senna led the two youngsters who had not been chosen from her home, commiserating with them as she left the room.

'Ye'll have another time this one t'wernt right for you' she said gently. The two; a boy and a girl were almost in tears. But the code of strict control under which we had been raised held them back;

they could allow their emotions be free once they were within the confines of their own homes; in public it was unthinkable.

Once the door closed behind them Senna returned to the chamber to observe the next phase of the bonding.

The pups were making friends with their chosen companions with much rolling on the floor, yipping and laughter. Jona and Caspa watched in approving silence. Then almost as one the couples broke off their play and sat face to face waiting for the next part of the ceremony.

Unusually, I had named my companion at the moment when we joined minds, knowing in that instance what the rikono wished to be called, but the others still had to name their pups.

Each of them in turn offered their new companion a name, if the pup agreed it would enthusiastically lick the youngster's face and the deal would be struck. If a pup disagreed it would simply sit and wait for a name it liked. Sometimes a naming could take all night. Without my ability to read minds, the others were at a disadvantage.

But it worked; the pup would only react if the name offered were to its liking. After all it was the one who would be responding to that name for the rest of its life so why shouldn't it be allowed an input?

MIND SPEECH

The pup was bounding in a straight line directly at me, crossing the shingle with much skittering and sliding. I was afraid the crazy run would end with broken legs, and called. 'keel it doon lad there'snae need to galopa such a lick.'

The pup ignored me in its exhilaration and ended its leggy run at my feet a few moments later, tongue lolling out of the side of its mouth. Tybot gave a huge smile and the impression 'found you my loved one' filled my mind.

~

Over the years leading up to my bonding with Tybot, I had spent much of my time learning to be the 'selected one.' It had been easy for me to 'speak' with the Raybaros seeing through their eyes and learning to communicate with them after they had 'opened' my mind.

Speaking telepathically to Q'asha and 'hearing' the other settlers was now to me as easy as normal speech. One of the Great Ones my mentor; Lord Dominie, mentally we had soared together my mind joined with his high over the snow capped Alban Mountains; in those moments I learnt to love the stark and awesome beauty of the land that had been named Arcadia by the Firster's.

A true Arcadia it was, beautiful and desolate, welcoming yet harsh, the Firster's had named it well.

At the end of my eleventh year, a few months after my bonding with Tybot the Raybaros shut themselves away from me. No matter how I tried they would only communicate with Q'asha, and then as before only from within the stone circle.

Initially I was distraught at the loss; it was as though my arms had both been hacked off. As the years passed so the pain diminished. I had so much I wanted to ask them, so many questions but no matter how much I pleaded, they held themselves aloof from me.

Initially I questioned Q'asha about my inability to communicate with them, but my questions were always answered with; 'Raybaros know fine, lass, time'll come they'll dit again. Dinna't mak it sich a sair chavv.'

Even though I more or less understood, I missed that astonishing mind to mind contact which had been mine since I had toddled my first steps.

~

When Tybot was four months old, a few weeks after his birth date, I felt he was ready, I entered his mind extending my own thoughts into the little rikono's sub consciousness, with a tiny 'tweak' I did for the rikono that which the Raybaros had done for me.

I opened the pup's awareness allowing him to understand and to communicate with the power of thought. Although Tybot had no speech he could understand both my spoken and my mental words, in return he was able to put across feelings and emotions that I swiftly learnt to interpret.

We now joined each with the other so intimately that we understand each other's innermost feelings, desires and reservations.

WALK IN THE FOREST

It was one morning a year later that I woke feeling different. I discovered a yearning scratching at my mind, a longing to travel further afield than our daily walks had previously taken us.

By now we had bonded almost completely, within our minds we had become almost as one. The rikono had developed a wicked sense of humour. Our crazy antics were more down to him than to me. Many were the good natured cries of abuse we had to endure after carrying out one of his carefully planned pranks.

That morning as the urge to explore became too strong to ignore, after morning meal, Tybot and I set off before anyone was up and about. We passed quickly through the gates acknowledging the sodjers as we went.

It was still snowing when we set off, but within moments the sun began peaking over the distant horizon turning the sea and the last few remaining clouds a bright pink. The niege which lay on the ground was almost up to my ankles it hadn't yet begun to melt. The Radgies had completed their usual disappearing act and all was quiet. Shenkies had marched the previous morning. We were clear to roam.

Tybot skipped across the cold pebbles, found a suitable spot for a xjin and relieved himself, watching with amusement as his stream turned the nege yellow. He gave a mental grunt of relief as he finished.

Clearly pleased to be outside the township walls so early in the morning he glanced at me, 'destination?' he queried,

'A vesh' I responded. The rikono now fully grown had lost most of the crazy exuberance of puppyhood, and rather than dashing off in the direction of the trees fell in alongside me and nosed my hand in a gesture of affection. Together we set off at a swift trot away from the walls, towards the distant dark line of trees.

It had been many years since anyone from the township had been far from the outer walls most were content to remain within the protection offered by their homes and the tall stane dykes. No one could remember anyone having been to the forest, even though the nearest trees were in full view of the township about two klicks distance. It was now somewhere that no one went or even wanted to.

As we came near to the massive trees with their flat topped spread of branches and large pulpy leaves, we could see areas around the base of each trunk where disturbed earth and chuckies, had been thrown aside leaving open scars with piles of overturned earth, stones and pebbles all around the boles.

We could see that the trunks of all the trees bore deep scars, they had been pierced in many places around head height, a clear liquid oozed from many of the fresh holes. In a moment of impetuousness I tasted it. It was sweet; letting it flow into my cupped hand I drank a handful of it. It was strangely refreshing and uplifting.

Tybot tried it and proffered his approval.

Above the deep puncture marks, the trunks were smooth and straight, stretching up towards the sudden spread of branches and leaves. Four men with their arms outstretched, fingertip to fingertip would be hard pressed to reach around one of the huge boles.

Tybot sniffed the broken ground at the base of a tree. I was in his mind and could taste the smells that flooded the rikono's senses 'aye Radgies' I agreed with the dog 'and scent a Shenkies too'.

Tybot grunted and moved to the next tree 'same here' he sent to me.

'I wonder what went on here' I mused, fingering one of the holes in a nearby tree trunk.

'Radgies' blood here, beloved' came the impression from the rikono.

'I smell it too' I replied.

We moved further into the trees, the sun's rays were blocked out almost immediately to be replaced by a green and eerie light. The sunlight filtered through the thick green canopy overhead. The light didn't penetrate completely leaving dark areas of deep shadow behind the bare trunks. Nothing grew in the spaces between the trees not even saplings; all the trees were identical in size, in shape and in height.

We moved a few more steps into the forest, both of us as cautious as the other. Almost every tree showed the same signs of root area disturbance and scaring at head height. I probed with my mind to search our surroundings for signs of life, immediately I found both Radgies and Shenkies. Both species were all around us under the ground. The Radgies were in deep underground tunnels and hollows, some of them were awake and moving about. The Shenkies however were totally immobile, and surprisingly were under our feet less than four feet deep, buried in the earth all around the boles of the trees.

Tybot used his nose in the same manner. 'I smell them, beloved' came the rikono's impressions, 'both been here, above ground, not long ago'.

Although he used no actual words the mind stream of feelings and emotions that came from the rikono conveyed his meanings and I understood perfectly.

'Not nice here' I said aloud my voice echoing strangely, 'let's gan back a sunshine, it be serious kalt' my voice sounding out of place in the silent forest.

The nege hadn't quite melted at the edge of the vesh, a sharp vent which was still blowing in from the sea across the little drifts which had built up along the edge of the forest cooled the wind until it was almost freezing. I had dressed only thinly, with lightly covered legs and arms, my cloak rode in a pack on my back. The Vesh had shadows, that were not only the darkest I had ever experienced and aside from the wind, had a touch that made me feel colder than I had felt in my life.

There was something else too something that I couldn't quite perceive, even with my senses at full stretch. I decided that discretion at this point was the better part of valour; it was time to vacate the dark forest. Of similar mind we turned together and made our way quickly back to the sunshine.

'Let's along the tree line' I said, without another word we began to walk. The silence and the strange sensations we had in the forest had left us both feeling subdued. At the time we didn't know it, but our walk that day became the beginning of the turning point for all the inhabitants of our settlement. A change rivalling that of the moment 'we' had arrived in the land, many generations before.

We travelled hugging the tree line for over an hour, it wasn't a gentle stroll for we moved rapidly. The ground all along the forest line was broken open, the chuckies and the earth, a clinging black loam in places, appeared freshly dug, and those spots smelt strongly of Radgies.

We found nothing other than that we had already encountered. However the further from the township we walked the less was the evidence of Radgies, of the Shenkies and the damage to the trees there was no change, a quick calculation of a small area revealed thousands of the buried horrors of all dimensions, ranging from the size of my hand to full grown.

The forest must be home to countless thousands, buried beneath the trees, every one of them was inert, devoid of any signs of life.

'Wonder what happens here' I thought, looking at the disturbed earth under a tree.

'They fight and kill each other, eat or be eaten' came back Tybot's impressions. I grimaced at the mental image the dog sent of Radgies and Shenkies fighting and eating each other.

'Losh' I shouted 'that's it, you got it heart of my heart, and how came you to be so clever?'

'Easy', came the joyful reply, 'I haven't any competition' he skipped sideways away from the playful swipe that I swung at him. 'Couldn't even catch a pup' he continued, sending an impression of me disappearing back into the distance as he loped away. With a yelp of amazement he found himself upended as I lifted him with the power of my mind, and tipped him over onto his back.

I had never accomplished moving anything quite so easily before, it had always required a conscious effort, but at that moment it seemed to happen as I wished.

I stood for a moment, shocked at what I had done.

'No fair' he complained, 'I can't do that, but I'm still faster than you'.

'Dinnae count on it,' I said.

THE TOMMY FIELDS

Our spirits began to lift almost immediately we left the oppressive dark green of the forest, and within minutes we were back to our usual relationship of fun and banter. I noticed that the tree line seemed to be following the shore at an exact distance all along its length, where the shore came in, or moved further out, the forest retreated or advanced in accurate measure.

My senses warned me it was approaching 'Fall time', I pulled my cloak from my backpack, and kirtled it round my shoulders, automatically flipping the hood over my head.

'You're covered' sent Tybot, giving an image of me covered from head to foot in mud, after he had completed a quick tour around me.

I chanced a quick glance at the sun to confirm my body clock's warning, the sun's aura was almost completely dark green, with my cloak and hood in place I stood and waited impatiently for the 'fall' to finish.

'Let's away', I said, 'Falls over'. 'I want to check around that next corner to see if there is anything different there before we turn back.'

The rikono looked at me quizzically, 'time is short, beloved, surely there can be nothing more than we have seen already' a final image of the sun setting and the Radgies rampaging around us both, said it all.

'I know' I responded, 'but I want a quick look round yon next bend'.

'Hurry then' replied the rikono.

We made our way to the curved edge of the forest, as we rounded the corner I was stunned by what I saw; an entire area more than a klick wide was full of strange plants 'what could they be?' I wondered. The closest were about twice my height and were covered in leaves; they gave off a strong, strange but pungent smell that by itself was not unpleasant. Each plant was festooned with bunches of red and green globes. Some of the bunches were almost close enough for me to reach.

On impulse I jumped and clung on to one of the smaller stalks swinging below it. With a snap it suddenly came away and I landed on my rump the stalk still in my hands.

I was slightly winded as I landed.

The globes were quite large, each easily as big as my head.

I climbed to my feet and pulled a quick painful gasp of air into my lungs.

'Clever trick that, what you going to do now?'

'Not funny, that hurt',

'I know, I felt it' sent the rikono,

'Not as much as I did'.

Tybot sniffed the globe, 'smells funny, what you think they are?' he sent.

I gently pressed against the red skin of one and was surprised not only by its softness but the strength of it. It was pliable to the touch. After a minute of pressing, squeezing, punching and poking the rubbery skin split with a gush of thick fluid that splashed across my face filling my open mouth. I spat it out, my wits reacting automatically to the sharp taste but a residue remained, apart from the strong tangy flavour I realized that it tasted wonderful.

I had never known anything like it. Having lived my entire life eating nothing but Mas flesh and the skimpy rations of root bobas; the stunted tatties and neeps that we cultivated in one corner of the township this was an amazing taste sensation.

Catching my thoughts Tybot tentatively licked my hand, and immediately made a 'yuk' with his mind. I wasn't convinced; I pulled off a small piece of the fleshy substance, popped it in my mouth and chewed. It was an explosion of taste. My eyes watered and I choked for a moment, but once I recovered I chewed the spongy pulp with renewed vigour, it was fantastic. I grabbed another handful and stuffed it in my mouth.

The rikono watched intently savouring the pleasure that I was experiencing but disinclined to try the red mush. After a few more handfuls I could eat no more my stomach felt heavy and slightly uncomfortable. I had never felt full before.

I looked around. The entire area within my field of vision was full of similar plants and many others which were totally different. The majority of the bushes and trees were easily as tall as I, and some much taller. Many were full of strange shapes some were green and others of so many colours that I had no names for.

The plants closest to me had coloured globes, all the way through the various shades of green to yellow and the bright red globes that were closest to me. There were many flowers I didn't recognize, I had only ever seen 'tattie floors' before and they were pale blue or yellow, these flowers were all the colours I had ever seen, and many others that I hadn't.

I had no experience of fruiting plants, so had no way of knowing what the different colours signified or even were. I stood gazing in amazement.

'Beloved, we need to go now' sent Tybot, breaking me from my daydream.

'Need to take some back' was my response, and I began scooping what remained of the red globe into my back pack first extracting my cloak. I noticed hard oval, yellow pieces in the softer juicer area of the globe. These oval pieces were almost the size of my own teeth. Without thinking why I added a few of them too, and then closing the pack over the red mushy mess, hefted it onto my back, 'let's go then' and I broke into a ground covering jog back towards the township.

I decided then to try to lessen my body weight using my mind in the same way that I had topsy-turvied Tybot. I felt my body lighten and within moments I was travelling fast, taking huge bounds across the beach.

Tybot initially stood still in shock but the running rikono was up to the challenge, and at full stretch managed to catch up with me. I knew he would tire quickly and with my mind reduced his weight until he was matching me step for step. I slackened my own speed slightly and we fell together into a phenomenal ground covering pace.

Within less than two hours we had come in sight of the township and within minutes were back at the gates. I ran through the maze and the turnstiles, Tybot still bravely at my heels.

Q'asha was waiting, for I had called her mentally as we approached the town.

I shrugged out of my pack's harness, 'Try this' I said excitedly, indicating the red mush that filled my pack. As if to demonstrate, I took a piece and crammed it into my mouth.

By now an intrigued crowd begun to gather, Q'asha tentatively took a small piece, sniffed it. The pungent smell wrinkled her nose but not to be outdone she slipped it in her mouth. The look of sheer pleasure that came over her face caused me to 'whoop' with excitement, I danced in a circle my hands clapping in the air.

The watching settlers had never seen such an exhibition, it being totally outside our austere way of life and harsh traditions against showing emotions, but my excitement seemed to be infectious and I was quickly joined in my impromptu dance by Tybot and some of the younger children. Together we were jumping and spinning round and round. The children not really understanding why but they enjoyed being caught up in my exhilaration.

Q'asha had by now taken and eaten a further handful of the pulp, she began passing the pack round for others to try. They came forward taking a tiny piece each, but it wasn't long before there were smiles all around, and questions were being fired at me.

'I'll show you in the morn' I began 'I be needing strong ones t' come with me, we'll be needin t'take some o' your yowies, an we's needin tows, take shivs, and ye'll be going a fair likt, so be up for it, we's startin' first light.'

Q'asha stood beside me adding her authority, for I was still a maiden in many eyes.

The settlers broke away, speculating excitedly and wildly on the origin of the globes, comparing it to raw Mas flesh in consistency, but with a much stronger, and more delicious, tangy taste.

Sunset was approaching, some of the fushmen among them would be needed to run the Mas and give protection against Shenkies, but before that; evening meals had to be eaten, the ceremony was traditionally completed by sunset, families always eating together. We had much to accomplish in the hours before dawn, for all of those who had tasted a small handful of the red mush were eager and wanted more. The strong and the fit amongst them couldn't wait to be a part of my expedition, to collect more of the delicious stuff whatever it was.

A TIME OF HARVESTING AND OPENING

'Q'rem' it was a mind call from Q'asha.

I gave her a quick, 'Aye, listenin' in response.

'I been searching through the Books, I think I know what you found but I can't be sure how they came to be on Brimat'.

'You said the plant has lots of green leaves, and has a strong smell, that the globes were green, yellow or red, with hard pieces inside, and a soft but coorse to break skin' she continued.

'I found something that seems to match, the strips show a plant that comes from another land, and they were commonly eaten all over either on their own or with other foods, they were called 'tomatoes' in Engls, and were known as 'fruit' they have many seeds inside. There is one thing I don't understand, they came in many different sizes, but the largest were only supposed to be as big as two clenched fists, and yet you say you couldn't put your arms around some you saw'.

'Let's wait till morning, and we'll check them out properly', I sent.

'Sounds best' she responded, 'Sleep well'.

'Aye, ye anall' I said aloud. Knowing she would still pick up my thoughts.

~

It was before dawn, as we waited for the Radgies to clear, the snow was still gently falling, and B'goi was dropping towards the far horizon for the culmination of its 'night's passage.' The fushmen had decided not to net for Mas, the elusive creatures had not shown on the shelf all night, and there was now no chance of them appearing, three yowies had been left to give protection against any passing creatures which might inadvertently cross the gap, the other two came ashore early.

I had thirty Brimatins, both men and women waiting to join me. They were all wearing light clothing; each had their alucloaks strapped to the top of back packs. They were among the strongest and fittest of our townsfolk.

My expeditionary force was made up in the most part by off duty fushmen and township guards, the sodjers, between them they carried six yowies and each of them carried Shenkie knives and lengths of rope.

My father was amongst the waiting men and women.

'Ta t'ee for cummin Pa,' I said.

'Think I'da missed this'n?' He said proudly 'I's richt ahind ye young'un, an nae mistake' he turned to his podna Jona, 'that'd be fae both on us'.

Jona nodded hefting his pack onto his back, 'aye' he muttered, 'I be pahreh.' Nodding to his podna, he lifted up one side of their boat, and waited as Tymoth picked up the other.

Jona hadn't tasted the pulp that I returned with, and although others had raved about it, he was convinced like many that the journey might do nothing other than put us all in danger and what use did the stuff have other than a nice taste.

I resisted going into my uncle's mind to reassure him knowing it was unnecessary; Jona was a fiercely loyal companion to us all. I knew that once he could see the benefits that the new food would bring to the township diet, I would be able to count on his total support.

The group set off, following Tybot and I. We kept our pace down, as the others would have never stood a chance of keeping up with us if we had adopted our speed of the previous evening.

Even so it took over four hours to reach the field.

I managed to keep our overall speed up by allowing the group frequent short stops to take sips of water and to catch their breath. All but the fittest were exhausted and almost in a state of collapse, all needing a rest which I allowed before we rounded the last corner of the forest, I collected some of the tree waters in a flask which greatly helped the most exhausted, who took a drink of it. I had found it necessary to mentally lift most of them at some part or other of the trip, decreasing their body weight so that they felt they were almost flying. None of them had ever been this far before. I calculated we had covered almost twenty five klicks from the township, they had done well. At a normal walking pace it would have taken us more than five hours.

We rounded the corner and the field came into view, gasps of amazement came from all around, with sudden renewed strength they ran forward towards the plants. Q'asha turned to me, 'you done good lass, thanks for the lifts, but think on, we still got to get them back before dark.'

'I've thought of that teacher, if you let me, I'll teach you the trick, and then you can help me get them all back.'

'Why don't we open them?'

'Are they ready?'

'You'll never know unless you try' she sent.

I thought for a moment 'I'll start with the oldest, which must be you'.

Q'asha swung an ear cuff that deliberately missed, and smiled, 'OK, go for it' she sent, 'won't be the first time you've messed about in my head.'

I closed my eyes for a second, initially Q'asha felt nothing, and then she became aware of a wriggling at the corner of her mind, with a flash of awareness she knew I had been inside her sub consciousness. I had given a little twist in one microscopic area, as the Raybaros had done for me, and it seemed to her as if I had turned the sun on inside her head.

She suddenly became aware of thoughts and unspoken words coming from all around as she stood with her eyes closed. 'Careful' I spoke into her mind, 'hold them out, focus only on the one you want, and close out the others, if you don't get a hold of them, like this, they will swamp you, and you will lose control of your own thoughts.' I showed her the technique that I had developed through those many painful moments when my mind had almost been overcome by the clamouring thoughts of others around me.

Q'asha knew what it was like to hear the Raybaros in her mind, that, and the years she had been communicating with me, enabled her to quickly master the technique I illustrated for her mentally; her opened mind now understood exactly what I meant.

'I think some of them might lose their minds if you do that to them without some training first'.

'I guess' I replied

'I'll start with a couple for this trip which should be enough to help get us back to the Township before nightfall tonight.'

'I'll need you to find at least three possible people - the most capable, and turn them, Tybot and I are going to have a quick look around the other side of this field'.

'I'll try'.

'OK'

I turned and set off in a high speed lope around the edge of the field; Tybot flew after me like a streak, those who noticed us leaving, many experts with their own running rikonos stood with mouths wide open watching the amazing display of speed from both of us.

Q'asha watched as we disappeared around the edge of the field, and then turned back to the task I had left her. She allowed her mind to drift across the settlers touching their minds, looking for those who had the strongest mind outputs. She was surprised to find that all of them were more or less equal and that they all had powerful latent abilities, some were almost as high as her own.

She called the nearest to her, 'Jona'

'Aye Keeper' my uncle responded stepping towards her.

'I'd like a couple a words, wi ye' she said, 'wannat tak lang'

The man's mouth and hands showed that he had at last sampled the fruit, 'This be amazin stuff, tastes affa fine.'

'Me knows. Come I've a task f'r ye'.

She took him to one side and explained asking his permission, Jona was surprised that the Keeper wanted his help, but said that he would allow her to do anything she wanted; he was open to her suggestions. Having had close contact with me throughout my life, he knew that whatever happened it would be life changing for him.

Q'asha did what she had to, to open his mind and promptly taught him how to filter and control the thoughts that flooded in. Jona went off by himself for a short while to master the new and amazing gift he had .received.

Q'asha decided that she would 'turn' as many of them as she could, then realizing that those she had already changed were in their turn able to pass on the gift. She enlisted them to do the same for their fellows. As instructions had been given mentally they were exactly replicated appearing in the recipient's mind as though they were actual memories. Within a few minutes all thirty volunteers had been opened.

The lives of us Smokies would never be the same again for those thirty would open their families and friends, and before long the entire township would have the gift.

She wondered if I knew that giving the gift to her would be the start of a chain reaction, she was sure I would approve but would the Raybaros she thought with a moment of trepidation.

Fruit picking and yowie filling was completed in a strange silence although there was a great deal of thought conversation going on as the thirty quickly mastered their new abilities.

By now it was almost 'fall' and Q'asha sent a thought to me, 'we'll be ready to move after fall.'

'OK' I replied, 'I see you've opened them all, any probs?'

'None'

'Maybe should've done it years ago'

'No, they wouldn't've been ready'.

'Losh bihere' was my reply, 'when you're ready start them back I want to have a proper look at something I've found' I sent a visual image of an object half buried in the chuckies and partially covered in plants, that I hadn't noticed the previous evening.

'OK, see you back home,' she sent as she played the image I had sent over in her mind, I caught her next thought too 'now is the time for her to learn to read the strips.'

I broke off my contact at that point leaving her to her thoughts. I decided to explore a bit before checking the object out. It was a massive container, totally black and oval in shape. I took a while walking all round it before Tybot and I decided to look further around the amazing field of plants.

We set off running at almost full speed covering the perimeter of the field down towards the sea shore in enormous weightless bounds. We rounded a bulge in the forest which was filled by the plantation of fruit plants. The rikono was thrilled to be running alongside me and for me to even outpace him something that had not happened since he was a pup. He threw down a challenge, 'think you're fast now, do you'?

'Yep' came my reply.

The rikono burst ahead with a blinding flash of speed. I smiled, and then sped off after him; 'To that tall plant then,' I sent an image.

'You better hurry, I'm almost there,' the joy of running was bubbling through the rikono's thoughts.

'I'm behind you.'

'Not possible.'

'I'm alongside you.'

The rikono yelped in surprise, as he glanced sideways and saw me, 'I give up, you're unreal' he sent.

We ran on revelling in our newly discovered speed and abilities.

I stopped running, almost instantly defying inertia, and raised my hand to my eyes shading the sun.

'What see you beloved'? The rikono was behind a small, bushy green plant with red flowers. I opened my mind to the rikono giving him the view seen from my slightly taller vantage point.

'I don't know what it is'

I passed my view to Q'asha she replied with genuine surprise tinged with recognition, and once again sent 'that it was time I read the 'strips' I was perplexed but noted her warning tone.

We moved forward at a walk towards the 'gi'huge' item that stood wedged amongst the rocks off the shoreline. It could have easily covered most of our settlement. I had nothing else to reference it against, and nothing in my experience could have prepared me for the sight.

We approached the structure Tybot moved off to the right whilst I continued forward in a straight line, my mind in turmoil. There was no way this could be a natural object, it had to have been built by something or someone but the sheer size of the object confounded me. It appeared to be a structure entirely made of our rarest of commodities, metal. It stood almost as tall as the forest trees that initially had hidden it from my view.

THE CREW

'Stand Still! - Don't move or we'll run you through!'

I spun round. Facing me were three strangely dressed people; two men and a woman. The men held sharp spears, and they were pointed directly at me.

'Who are you?' I asked in Engls as that was the language with which I had been addressed. I was torn between disarming them with my mind and letting them think that they had me captive. I allowed capture to win in order to find out more about them. I could not understand why other humans should be offering me harm; it was not the way of my people.

'No' said the woman brusquely, 'who are you?' she spoke Engls with a strange inflection that I had never heard before.

I stood still assessing the trio, they had long brown shoulder length hair, dark brown eyes, and their bodies were covered in a tan coloured, medium length fur. Apart from the palms of their hands, and I guessed the soles of their bare feet, which were clear of any fur and pure white. They wore lightly woven shorts and open sleeveless tops clipped at the waist. Unlike us who wore our hair short,were blue eyed, olive skinned and entirely free of any body hair. We, as our principles dictated wore long sleeved chemises and ankle length trousers, with baffies covering our feet. I was slightly embarrassed seeing the men with open shirts.

I guessed the men's ages to be around nineteen with the woman a year or two older, they were all at least a head shorter than I.

As they assessed me in like manner, Tybot casually strolled up and took his place beside me. Instantly their demeanour changed.

They looked incredulously at him in total awe verging on reverence in their eyes.

'Is that a real dog?' said the woman quietly.

'Yes' I replied, placing my hand on Tybot's head and gently squeezing his ears in a gesture of affection.

The spears dropped; the two men stepped back and fell to their knees bowing their heads, leaving the woman to speak.

'I have never seen a real dog before,' she said in a whisper sinking to her knees as well, although her eyes remained fixed on Tybot.

'Why are you kneeling?' I asked.

'Because people with dogs are to be our saviours, we know that one day they will come back to rescue us from the killers'.

'The killers?' I was perplexed 'what are they?'

'They come at night, they fight the black beasts which come from out of the ground, the killers eat anything, any fruit that has ripened and fallen to the ground.'

I guessed the killers to be Radgies, and the black beasts could be none other than our dear friends the dreaded Shenkies.

'We cannot leave the ship after dark for fear of being attacked. In the past our ancestors would fight against them. But there were many, many losses. We now spend each night on board in our cabins. We have no other protection,' she waved at a nearby ramshackle wooden structure 'this old fort was built by our ancestors, but failed to give true protection, the killers would tunnel beneath the walls.'

'Fall is due, I must cover up,' I said, pulling my cloak from my pack and covering my head and the exposed skin of my hands.

Concerned that the others took no action, I asked why.

'We have no need' the woman said watching my actions closely.

'My name is Q'rem, and this is Tybot' I said from under my hood.

'I am Annar,' she made no introductions for the men who had remained in their positions of deference; motionless throughout the time we had been speaking.

'Where are you from and where are your women leaders?' She asked abruptly. I slipped into her mind to discover what she meant by the word 'leader'.

'Our women are not our leaders, we are all equal, but my mother's father has a final say in any disagreements, if that can be called a leader. Although he has not undertaken mediation duties for many a year. Our Keeper Q'asha is perhaps an elder of sorts but we have no one who is a leader. I come from a settlement which is about six to eight hours walk from here.'

She kept asking questions as we began walking, until I, exasperated by the continual harping gently slipped into her thoughts, what I found there surprised me. She had a mental latency which when opened would rank her alongside any of the settlers in ability.

I withdrew and said with my mind, 'Do not be afraid, you are not imagining it, I am talking to you in your mind. I can explain all I know and all about Fort Brimat and my people in a moment, if you will allow me.'

Her eyes opened wide in astonishment as she became aware that I was speaking in her thoughts she nodded quickly, 'I would like to know' she said aloud, 'But first let us go inside the ship and you can tell the other women at the same time.'

She turned with a quick look at Tybot, 'You are beautiful' she said.

'Thank you,' sent the rikono.

She gave a gasp as she realized that the dog had spoken inside her mind his thoughts were feelings and emotions, she knew that it had not been me, for I created what she perceived as spoken words.

I walked beside the woman around a bend in the forest of plants, and saw it in its entirety, standing off from the shoreline. It was the biggest single thing I had ever seen in my life; it was enormous larger even than our whole settlement, and it stood higher than the tallest trees. It filled my entire horizon.

Climbing a waist high gap between the chuckies and the edge of a rough wooden bridge, we made our way up a long swaying ramp which crossed a wide stretch of water. The men followed adroitly behind.

'We have cabins for the men in the lower decks,' she volunteered, pointing to the rows of round holes, we women have our cabins on upper deck. 'I would like to know how your people have survived without the protection of a ship.'

'I will explain all to you when we get to where we are going.'

She gave me a look that suggested she was used to instant obedience, and was having problems controlling herself from reprimanding me, after all I was but a mere maid, no more than sixteen she guessed; her own men folk of my age would have been severely punished long before now. I had even had the impudence to look straight into her eyes when I spoke, and as for the idea that men were equal to women, and the strange way I could speak into her mind caused her a great deal of indignation, as well as not a little apprehension.

I continued to monitor her mind amused at the bewilderment that was underlying all her feelings.

'You may come to my cabin, and we will speak there first,' she said trying to regain control. We had come to a stop in a huge room, the walls were lined with precious and beautiful wood; I could not believe the magnificent treasures all around me.

'No, I would prefer to speak to all of your people, both men and women at the same time, arrange for them to be brought here immediately.' She began to object strongly, but found herself looking into my eyes. For a moment her senses began to swim and she felt dizzy. She turned to her male companions and gave the order I had implanted in her mind.

'Fetch all the others' she commanded.

The two men turned and ran to do her bidding; it was some twenty minutes before the entire population of the 'ship' the 'crew' as they called themselves were assembled in front of Tybot and I. The men looked subdued almost frightened but the entire 'crew' had bowed reverently to Tybot as they passed in front of him, much to his amusement, he had nick-named them 'little fluffies.'

OPEN THE MEN

I was devastated to find the 'crew' numbered in total less than a hundred souls, but it pleased me to see that a good number of them were children - some even babes in arms. Obviously the reason behind their tiny population was not down to the lack of children.

I scanned their minds as they passed me and was pleased to find they all had the same latent mental abilities, clearly they were as ready as my people were to be 'opened'.

The adults, even the tallest of the men, were all slightly built. All of them shorter than I. Even my ma was taller, and she was a 'shortie' I thought with a smile.

They assembled in a wide open space in front of me in silence waiting for me to speak. The men and boys were at the placed at the back of the gathering, the women and girls assuming positions at the front.

'Q'asha, I be in need of help' I sent, opening my eyes and mind to her, and replaying the sequence of events leading up to that moment.

I then began speaking to them, my voice loud and clear and hopefully I sounded confident. First I asked them to sit. When they eventually complied, the women muttering and complaining, I began by introducing himself and Tybot.

I then recounted to them, fed information by Q'asha, of the people of Fort Brimat, in less than half an hour I had given them a potted history, emphasizing the equality of men and women, and the companionships we shared with our dogs.

'What you say is difficult to believe how can we be sure it is true?' came a haughty question from one of the women at the front. Her mind gave the information in response to my quick scan that she was leader of the 'crew' the others deferring to her as 'Cap'n'.

"Cos I say it is'.

Heads spun in unison towards the source of the new voice.

Q'asha pushed through the doors into the room; an impressive sight, standing a head taller than I, which towered her above 'the little fluffies.' Her black cloak with its hood up, covering her unique dark hair made her seem even taller. As she strode towards them she appeared to float across the floor; the only sound was the swishing of her cape.

'Jonaan your dad, taken 'em back' she sent to me.

'Okay, what we gonna do with these 'uns?'

'Open them' it seemed Q'asha wanted to share her new found experiences with everyone.

'I'd a thought on 'at but yon cyard stopped me.' I glanced at the Cap'n.

'Open men then.'

I glanced away from her for a moment not believing her thoughts, looking at the anxious downcast faces of the men across the heads of the no less shocked women.

'We can then do women when balance be richt', she finished.

The exchange had taken moments; Q'asha was still striding across the vast floor which was made of the same plush wooden material as the walls and ceiling.

'You men and boys go with Q'rem, I want to speak with the women,' she commanded.

This is more like it, thought Annar, a woman, even one as tall and scary as this one, is in charge of them. If it hadn't been for Tybot's presence, that girl would have been beaten for her impudence.

The ship's women relaxed and waited impatiently for their men to exit which they did almost at a run and in complete silence, I followed Tybot padding along beside me.

I must admit I was concerned, would generations of dominance by women set off a backlash amongst the men once their abilities had been enhanced to what could only be regarded as superhuman. Only time would tell, but I was appalled at the violent reprimands and even beatings which had been meted out at the merest whim even by the youngest of girls, and the slave like attitudes of the men and boys which I had gleaned from the thoughts of the forty or so males who preceded me from the stateroom.

That had to stop; hostility against another was unheard of amongst us for we had enough violence from outside our walls to contend with. That was the concept I decided to instil in their minds 'deal with the aggression outside' life was too precious to waste, damage or destroy.

Once we had reached the ship's ramp I called for them to stop and sit in a semi-circle on the deck in front of me. As I was female they complied without hesitation; I began by casting my mind across theirs looking for the strongest latent.

A young man stood out from the others by a small amount I called him by name, 'Ritchie, come here please' the man stood up, he was slim, almost boyish in stature like the others. His eyes, after first registering surprise at my knowing his name, looked directly into mine, quickly fell away in deference. He made his way swiftly towards me and stood in front of me eyes focusing in the distance.

'Look into my eyes, and don't be afraid.'

'Yes mistress, err, sorry miss' the man stumbled having given his usual response.

'I am no mistress of yours,' I said, 'I want you to relax, stop being so stiff and uptight.'

Ritchie relaxed visibly in response to my softly spoken words, in that instant I turned his 'lights' on, then began quickly pouring into his mind the precautions and protection techniques necessary to stop him from going mad.

Moments after Ritchie was 'open' I became aware of how perceptive mentally the man had instantly become, when he sent, 'teach me all of it, please,' looking straight into my eyes.

'Soon friend, right now I'm going to open the others.'

In less time than it had taken for us to walk from the meeting room to the top of the bridge, all the men had been opened.

Q'asha and I had decided not to open the boys.

I agreed with Q'asha at fifteen years old, which was the age at which a boy was deemed to be a 'crewman' as being the cut off.

I was sure that any of them who were younger than fifteen could suffer mental problems. Although I had been only four years old when the 'Raybaros' opened me, these youngsters were too intimidated to be ready for the enormous mental powers that they would receive.

Once they were accustomed to equality with the women, they should be able to endure the mental changes. Soon the twenty five opened men had become acquainted with their new abilities and felt confident in using them. I gave them all the new skills that they could cope with except one. In agreement with Q'asha, I withheld the knowledge of how to open others.

When I had finished, and they were ready I led them back into the stateroom; we had been away less than half an hour. Q'asha had passed the time answering questions.

There was surprise and annoyance among the women when the men returned 'Go back to your own quarters we are having an important discussion here that does not concern you,' ordered the Cap'n.

'No longer Cap'n,' replied Ritchie, 'Whatever happens here concerns all of us now not onlyyou women.' He stood without the customary bowed head looking her directly in the eyes.

'Impudence!' She shouted, and made to slap his face. In a movement that was so fast it could hardly be seen, he caught her wrist before the blow landed.

'Never again Lady, never again will you abuse us, from now on you will treat men as equals.' He stood holding her arm in a grip of steel, his eyes fixing hers. After a moment she looked away unable to hold his power filled gaze, tears of frustration running down her face.

'I think it's time we left lass, it will be nightfall in two hours', Q'asha turned back to the women, who were still trying to impose their will upon the unresponsive men.

'Sisters!' she said her voice ringing around the room, 'listen to your men folk they have the answers you have all been afraid of for so long. Listen to them, and learn to live together correctly as it should be, we shall return in a seven-day.'

With that we three;maid, woman and dog, turned and without further goodbyes left the ship at a fast run, disappearing in moments.

'You's gonna start on the books in the morn lass, there be a rite muckle you needs to know!'

'I need to know where that crew came from, for starters,' I responded.

'That you surely will, now let's see how fast we can get back home, I'd like to try to be there the same time as the others they only have about two hour's start on us', she chuckled.

'Hoik up yer britches then teacher, you's better lairn t'fly' I called over my shoulder as Tybot and I took off at our

130

astounding pace. She quickly assimilated the technique to lighten herself, which I mentally passed back to her. She amazed us, by matching us stride for stride. I must admit I had expected to have to lift her, and we had only taken off at such a lick as a prank.

LEARNING TO READ

It was the following day as I lay on a vissicouch in the 'Learnin' house next to Q'asha's dome, my eyes becoming accustomed to the dim light level.

'Open up yer mind lass, it's time for you a gilabav from books n strips' said Q'asha.

In the early days whenever I visited Q'asha, which was almost every day, using the blossoming power of my mind, I would smoothly increase the intensity of the lamp by imperceptible levels, turning up the wick and seeing how bright I could get it before Q'asha realized, and gave me 'that' look.

Q'asha placed the first book in front of me, leaning it against a stand; the book, she said was the first in a series that recounted the narrative of the exit of our people from Alba. The book was made from a material not unlike the alucloaks that we all carried to protect ourselves from the 'fall,' but where our oocloaks were velvety and pliable the books were stiff and hard.

It was covered all over in black shapes and squiggles; I peered at the markings trying to make sense of them. Knowing that Q'asha could extract amazing information from them, I felt discouraged that they showed me nothing.

~

'First me's needin t' lairnt yer to gilabav, guess I shuda done it ages past.'

Reaching out with her mind to mine, Q'asha began explaining the strange markings to me, showing me the word forms, deciphering the swirls and lines until I began to see words, and follow them as she read from a book taken randomly from one of the shelves, it took two days before I was able to competently read the script which Q'asha told me had been printed.

Once I could read without prompting, my ability, and my level knowledge grew exponentially. It was a frightening but illuminating account, and gave me an understanding of the origins of my people before they were interred.

It had taken me two days to read the first part but after a week I had finished 'The History of Mankind' with ease. A lot of it made little sense, but the learning experience was useful.

On the fifth day I began to read Andru Carne's journals, which told the stories of how the Firster's had initially come to Fort Brimat.

Six days out of the seven that the 'crew' had been promised passed, Q'asha and I were due our return visit the following day. Two further trips had already been undertaken over the past six days, to the 'fruit fields' as we had named them. Intentionally no contact had been made with members of the crew.

The tomatoes and other fruit and edible plants, were now fast becoming a welcome addition to our previously austere diet of 'Mas' flesh and root bobas. There was more than sufficient of the giant vegetables to go round.

Everyone in the township over the age of fifteen, had been opened, our lives were changing radically. Nothing will ever be the same again.

I was loathe to postpone my reading to accompany Q'asha, and suggested that in my place, she take my uncle Jona and his putain Caspa as her escorts. If anyone would be able to discipline those little Musstik women it would be my tall muscular uncle, by virtue of his size and looks alone. In reality Jona was as soft and gentle as Caspa, except of course, when it came to facing Mas and Shenkies with a spear in his hands.

So it was that I began to read my ancestor Andru Carne's journals. Andru's journal was written by hand, but after a while I managed to read the journal as easily as I had the printed book.

RITCHIE AND ANNAR

I had been pouring over the journal for most of the day, but stopped as Q'asha came into the dome.

'F'like?' was her greeting.

'Amazin' I replied. 'Me kens yon Firster's hat sair chaave, but nae so dur as thir strips dit.'

'Far ee up til?'

I showed her, 'Andru has spoken to the leaders,' I said.

'Losh, you done good getting as far as you have, but you've still got lots to go. Now it's time for evening meal, you can get back to the strips again tomorrow.'

'Fit happened at Ark?'

'Tell ee after soopa.'

~

I ran across the courtyard to my own home. I could hardly contain myself through the ritualistic meal, as soon as we had drunk water I excused himself from the table, and this time with Tybot at my heels I ran back across to Q'asha's dome. I announced myself mentally, and on her response pushed the door open. It was beginning to get dark.

I walked into the room, and was surprised to see Ritchie and Annar sat on the couch, 'I think these two can explain a little better than I can,' said Q'asha.

Ritchie and Annar stood to give me a welcome hug. Annar then threw her arms round Tybot's neck he stood rigid for a moment but the tip of his tail told another story. He seemed to have taken to the little Musstik woman.

'If we meld you will know everything immediately,' Ritchie said.

I was apprehensive; I had never even allowed Q'asha unrestricted access to my mind. A mind meld would mean that, a complete join in both directions. What would it be like? Could I hold back anything? Especially the parts where I had connected minds with the Raybaros as a child, I had always kept those moments a deep secret, it was what the Raybaros had wished. I wasn't prepared to break that charge.

At that moment I decided against allowing unrestricted access to my memories in return for knowing everything the crew had ever experienced.

'I cannat allow a mind meld,' I said, 'but you tell your story, that'll be fine.'

'These stories have been passed from generation to generation,' Ritchie began, 'there are those amongst us who are expected to memorize them word for word, it is our way of remembering our history.'

As he was talking, Ritchie seemed to slip into a waking dream as he rolled the memories back into his mind. His speech changed, he seemed to be concentrating less on his own memories and it became as though he was recounting the story from first hand.

'Our experiences are limited to our way of life and the stories of previous lives that have been lived,' he continued in a more positive tone we know nothing of technology.

'We are an indomitable people, resolute some might say. Well we have had to be, we have always been able to take most things in our stride. Coming from a land where the maximum daytime temperature hardly ever rises above freezing, and at night it falls well below. We lived our lives in homes made from frozen snow; we were known as Eskimos, although amongst ourselves we prefer Inuit.'

He slipped back to his own voice for a moment 'But I better tell you what I know of our history.'

'Ours was an aboriginal people; we mostly lived in the coastal Canadian Arctic, in Alaska, and in Greenland. We are related to the Yupik of Alaska and north-eastern Siberia.'

'We were abandoned in the year 1990, by unscrupulous people, who were interested only in our money, our goods and our equipment.' He had slipped back into the voice of his memories, 'We were making our way to join with another faction of our people who had taken refuge in Northern Scotland, and had with us everything we owned. Our ship was thrown up onto the rocks and smashed by a horrendous hurricane. Many of us, including the criminals were killed. Those of us who survived scrambled away from the ship as it was tumbled over by the wind. We were left with nothing but the clothes we stood up in. During that terrible first day before the skies went dark, we searched for refuge, finding nothing we were forced to take shelter in a large cave.

'We had been thrown back into the stone age, in fact we were worse off than stone age dwellers, they after all had weapons, they knew the land they lived in, they were a part of their environment, they knew how to survive, we had nothing and knew nothing about the environment we had been dumped into.

'We assumed that we had been abandoned in some uninhabited corner of Greenland, a misnomer if ever one existed. The ship had been beached on a rocky coast, the ground bare and frozen.

'There were about five hundred of us, men and women, old and young, husbands and wives, even children, some were not much more than babies. We huddled together in that cave as the temperature dropped to some unknown level, all we could do was to try to hold on to life, to survive, even if it was for one night.

'We had no food; we didn't even have the means to warm ourselves, to light a fire, or for that matter anything to burn. It was a freezing cold morning that first morning, there had been a gradual lightening of the sky outside the cave mouth, a biting wind blew outside the cave, and a watery sun finally rose for us to discover that fifty of our number had died of hyperthermia during that long and cold first night. The oldest, the most infirm, and some of the children had passed. It was impossible to bury them without tools, for the ground was too hard, so we placed their frozen bodies in a large side chamber until we could find some way of laying them to rest.

'After moving the bodies, the fittest amongst us divided into six groups of ten, our task was finding something to eat and somewhere to live, or we were finished.

'Another six groups of about the same numbers made their way down the hillside from the cave to look for anything that would burn. From the cave mouth we could see a clump of bushes which should provide something combustible, and even some dry sticks which we could rub together to make fire, or so someone had suggested.

'We were lucky, not only had we found shelter in the huge cave, we had found some dry bushes, a hard scrubby vegetation, with branches which we tore off, we even found some dead trees which were further down in the valley, we dragged them all up the hillside to a ledge by the mouth of the cave, the fire makers knuckled down to ignite the wood, and believe it or not they actually succeeded. It took them a couple of hours of frustrating and frantic rubbing, but that first little wisp of smoke was received like a reprieve from a death sentence, a ragged cheer rose from those watching as a tiny flame flickered.

'We had warmth. Fires spread all round the cave as others took burning branches with them, thankfully the cave had an opening high up which acted as a chimney, and the smoke was drawn up towards the ceiling.

'By the light of the flickering flames we could at last see the inside of our new home.

'We were in a huge space of cathedral like proportions, but at least it was dry, we had heard the sound of water flowing all night, and by the light from the fires we found the source, at one side of the cave ran a little stream, the water was potable, in fact it was almost sweet to the taste.

'We the hunters were lucky, we had armed ourselves with straight sticks, stones to throw and smash with, but we didn't even know if the land had anything which was edible, or even if it had any animal, we expected polar bears and seals, but no such luck. We tried the spiny leaves on the conifers that remained standing in the valley, but they were bitter and totally inedible, maybe if they were cooked they would soften a bit, but what could we cook them in? Now that was another question.

'At the bottom of the valley where many fallen trees were found, we came across some animals, they resembled rabbits, but without long floppy ears, they were about the same size as rabbits in America, so that is how we named them.They had no fear of us, there were thousands of them, we picked up as many as we could carry.

'Those left behind took no notice as we departed with their kin, even if we had walked off with a few hundred, the numbers remaining did not even seem to diminish, in fact it seemed as though more had taken their place.

'A sharp twist of the neck was sufficient to dispatch them, the difficulty was gutting and stripping the little bodies but 'where there's a will there's a way,' we managed to sharpen some sticks by rubbing them against the rocks, and chip some flint to create sharp edges, it was enough to split their bellies and we cleaned out their insides with snow.

'We cooked them over the open fires, run through on the end of green sticks, even so; smoked, scorched, almost raw, stringy, and with bits of burnt fur sticking to the meat, they tasted wonderful.

'Mind you by the next morning we knew that more care would have to be taken over our cooking, our empty insides rebelled in the most obvious of fashions. Squatting with ones nether regions exposed over a freezing hole that has been chipped out with a blunt stick in the icy ground, or no hole, depending on the urgency of the visit. Cleaning one's self with sharp spiky leaves is an experience that one only wants to have on rare occasions, not ten to twenty times a day.

'As the days passed we become more proficient, and able to survive, though we suffered many deaths. We began chippingmore flint to make knives and tip our spears, we began making clothing from the furry rabbit skins, we made coverings and beds from them as well, we found ways of cooking them which didn't cause dysentery, or maybe we became accustomed to their flesh.

'We became total carnivores, at first we were all ill, from the pure meat diet, but the vegetation was inedible, apart from a some frozen roots which we roasted in the ashes, they were chewy but edible. It was all there was to eat, but our bodies adapted to it, the human body is a wonderful thing in that it can adapt to its environment. We survived. It was difficult at first, but we survived, and we improved as the years without sun passed, then generations passed, we lost count of the years, it seemed as though we had lived in that place forever.

'We adapted, or maybe we regressed, we began to grow tight, dense hair all over our bodies which helped to keep out the constant biting cold. By now we had spread across the entire valley, we had taken over neighbouring caves. Our numbers were up to a few thousand before the separations. We directed our worship to the face of the broken moon.

'Different clans and groups evolved, self perpetuating and governing, with differing ideals, moving away from the original cave. But we were still in the Stone Age, living in caves, using stone implements, scratching in the ground to survive, eventually we became masters of the icy valley, we called Artica. Sometimes disagreements arose between the caves, and open and bloody warfare broke out. Those were difficult times, many died in the unnecessary wars. Eventually peace reigned when all the clans were united under one female despot; it has been so ever since, females are our rulers.

'We have never been able to progress further; we had nothing except the stunted spiny trees and the continuously multiplying bunnies which lived quite happily on the leaves. There were a couple of occasions awhile ago, perhaps three centuries, when a creature, a huge flying beast, visited our area, flying low across the settlements.

'We had expeditions outside the valleys but found nothing. Nothing grew, nothing lived, walked or slithered. The only habitable place was our green valley.

'Over the millennia the world began to change.

'The sun began shine baking the ground by day, freezing under the moon by night. Plants appeared almost overnight in profusion, around the caves and even the valley. Iit was difficult for most of us to adjust, as I said before, we were people who had lived a stone age existence for a tremendous length of time, how long no one knew.We had lost the ability to read and write, our speech was almost lost too, words that had meanings for anything outside our simple existence had been lost from our language as being unnecessary, after all what was the use of having words and expressions for things that hadn't been seen or experienced for thousands of years.

'We have always had a simple belief though; we have revered the only creatures other than ourselves that had been abandoned on the hillside above our main cave, three male dogs which belonged to one of thefirst men.

'In the early days they lived amongst us and were loved by all, but sadly after they died of old age we placed their bodies in a spot where they would be frozen for all time, they are still there, a little worse for wear. 'The glacier moves slowly, those three dogs are now about a two hundred yards further down the mountain from where they were first encased in the ice. 'We have always believed that when the lost people with their dogs came back into our lives we would be rescued.'

Ritchie broke off his lengthy monologue, exhausted, 'May I rest now, perhaps I can conclude this recounting at another time.'

I must admit to being disappointed as I had been totally engrossed, but I must admit the young man looked on the verge of collapse, so I was happy to wait for a later date when he could resume his tale.

THE MELDING

'So you have no idea how amazing the sight of your dog was,' he said in his own voice, sipping at a cup of tree water, which perked him up immensely.

'And to us when we saw Tybot last six day,' said Annar.

'How did you end up on the Ark?' I asked, 'And how did you learn so much, you say your ancestors were illiterate?'

'A number of people who had been on a scouting expedition when the world blossomed, returned after a few weeks, they found what you have seen, the remains of our ship stuck in the rocks. How it survived we have no idea. Many of us decided to move there to take advantage of it.'

'There is an extensive audible library on the ship and many small players were found which are solar powered, and which we used have comprehensively. Working out how they operated took our ancestors almost fifty years.' Annar filled in.

'I think that's enough for now lad,' said Q'asha, 'you need to read quite a few more pages of Andru's strips to give you a better background, and the rest of Ritchie's story can wait until another time I can see he is tiring.'

'And you will be seeing a lot more of us anyway,' said Annar, 'we are all moving into the empty homes here in the settlement,' she ended with a huge smile.

'Wow, I can't believe it,' was all I could say, even though I realized it was the logical solution, we had room and safety, they were in danger every night they spent in the ship.

'You better, 'cos it's true.'

I hugged them all; my heart was full of love for these strange little people even though I had only known them for a short while.

Tybot was hugged by Annar, he touched minds with Q'asha and Ritchie, and then we were out and walking slowly home, I was deep in thought.

~

'That's a cute couple of 'fluffy puppies' joining us' sent Tybot.

'What do you think about it?'

'I don't really know, could be a good thing, but they got an awful lot to learn, and quickly too, a bit too much of the old worship Tybot thingie though, I don't fancy too much more of that, it's a bit over the top.'

'You love it you old softie'

'Yeah, nice at first, but there can be too much of a good thing, I've had it most of today while you been pouring over those books, find out anything interesting?.'

'You wouldn't believe it.

'Try me.'

'You saying you want a mind meld?'

'Why not, it's about time someone tried it, why not us.'

'I know but the Raybaros said it was not allowed.'

'You were five then,'

'Yeah, and how old are you?'

'I mature quickly,' Tybot quipped.

'After 'night drink', we'll give it a try, any problems and we stop straight away OK?'

'Great!'

~

'Me piav pani' I said and drank the tas of water in one.

Thinking about our intended merge, I had a twinge of trepidation, and held back for a moment, but the rest of the family were ready to finish the soopa ceremony and I had to comply.

The 'night drink' lovoro was over all too quickly for me, but Tybot was fidgeting as if it had taken forever.

'Why all the rigmarole, I eat and drink if I want to.'

'That's why you make so many stinkies.'

Tybot didn't bother answering and retreated behind a wall of silence pretending to sulk; I couldn't help but notice the tinge of humour that lingered round my companion's closed off mind.

'Gotcha,' I laughed.

It was a short time later we ran down the stairs to my 'lair.'

'Ee sure bout is?'

'Yep' responded the dog.

We both bounced onto the sleep couch, Tybot lay with his head on my lap. I felt him tingling with excitement all over my own body.

I matched my breathing with the rikono's, then when I felt the time was right, when all was quiet I reached out with my mind, I extended a tendril of my consciousness deeper than I ever had before, memories of Tybot's puppyhood flooded into my mind. Quickly I sorted through them, putting them into chronological order, straightening out misinterpretations and misunderstandings from the time before he had been 'opened.'

The dog lay perfectly still, but I could feel his awareness watching me, watching as his beloved absorbed and rearranged his innermost feelings, memories and thoughts.

Once I had completed my journey through Tybot's mind I asked.

'Do you really want to carry on with this?'

'I'm with you beloved,' the rikono replied.

I then continued, extending my own meld slowly, exposing layer by layer of my own memories. I monitored Tybot's ability to absorb my own memories feeding him year by year from the beginning of my ability to remember. I reached the time when we first bonded, the flood of love that I had felt for the tiny pup when we first met welled up in me.

Without warning Tybot suddenly began to shiver. He shook uncontrollably from head to tail, and started to howl. A howl that went on and on and froze my heart, the enormity of my love for him, mixed with his own not inconsiderable love for me, had overloaded his mind.

~

I pulled my mind back quickly but I was too slow. The rikono continued to shudder and shake, howling inconsolably or so it seemed, then he suddenly went stiff and silent, his breathing fell away quickly until all that was left was an uneven panting. His tongue was hanging far out of the side of his mouth. He was so quiet I almost wished he would start howling again.

I was in a blind panic. I considered the fact that I might have killed or mentally destroyed my beloved companion. I tried to reach him with my mind but all I could discover was deep black mud where once was that vibrant, exuberant and enquiring mind.

'Help me!' I screamed mentally, without thinking I employed my basic level of thought sending, emotions and images that I would utilize during my childhood days, before I was properly opened, the level of thought transfer that I used when I communicated daily with the Raybaros.

'Oh please help me!'

Nothing!

In desperation I called Q'asha, using the person to person channel of mind-speech we had perfected. Although she was no further forward in her knowledge and ability than I at least she could give support.

Within moments she came running across the courtyard, pushed the door open and with no more than a swift nod at my wide mouthed mother. My father had already left for he had fishing duties at the gap. She was puffing a little as she ran down the stairs to my lair, her hair and clothing were dishevelled, she had obviously jumped straight from her bed.

In moments I had explained all to her. Tybot lay stiff, still panting heavily, she was as much in the dark as I as to what action to take.

We decided to call the Raybaros with joined minds, calling out as one, Q'asha had not communicated with them since I had opened her mind, maybe they would respond to us, even though she wasn't within the burial circle.

Together with our now conjoined minds we called for the Raybaros to hear us.

'DON'T SHOUT SO LOUD, WE CAN HEAR YOU FROM THE OTHER SIDE OF THE PLANET,' came a powerful reply, seemingly from close by.

'We need your help,' sent Q'asha, opening our minds to the Raybaros who had replied.

'SO THE PUP IS TOO FULL OF LOVE, THAT'S A GOOD THING, BUT IT WAS TOO MUCH FOR HIS LITTLE EMOTIONS TO HANDLE.'

I CAN HELP, Q'REM, YOU MUST GO BACK TO THE POINT IN YOUR MELD WHEN HE OVERLOADED, AND THEN OPEN YOUR MIND TO US TO FOLLOW THE PATH.'

I did as I was bid stumbling through the black pit of Tybot's mind searching for the exact spot.

I began to despair all was black, every part I passed through was dark and muddy - but then in one tiny place I found a faint glimmer of light. A glimmer of love, I knew I had found Tybot again.

I felt the Raybaros follow my mind link; the power of the mind that walked in my mental footsteps was almost too much for me to stand. I now understood the full significance of our foolish and impulsive act, and the reason the Raybaros had advised me all those years ago against opening my mind completely to another.

It was too dangerous for minds of different abilities to meld; the greater could easily swamp the lesser, leaving the lesser with a mind that had been wiped clean, leaving the lesser with 'a blank slate'.

The Raybaros lifted all of Tybot's memories and experiences from my mind, and fed them back into HIM, at the same time teaching the technique of mind repair to me.

The Raybaros withdrew its mind with the words, 'NOW YOU KNOW WHY WE SAID MELDING WAS SOMETHING TO BE WARY OF, BUT YOU KNOW NOW HOW TO TAKE THE NEXT STEP, I AM LEAVING. YOU HAVE THE ABILITY AND THE KNOWLEDGE TO FINISH THIS TASK.WE SHALL SPEAK SOON, HAVE NO FEAR, YOU HAVE NOT BEEN UNWANTED ALL THESE YEARS, YOU NEEDED TO LEARN IN YOUR OWN WAY, BE SURE THAT WE ARE WELL PLEASED WITH YOU.'

As quickly as it had arrived, the Raybaros' mind contact was gone.

I reflected on my contact with that great mind, I realized now that the Raybaros did not have the power of speech, they communicated in the same way as Tybot, with impressions and feelings.

They had a great deal of 'hot blood' in their thoughts, they were natural killers, fearsome hunters that had progressed to a level of high intelligence, but they had been hunter killers in the past, and they still were now.

Bringing myself back to the task in hand, I went back into Tybot's mind, all seemed to be in place, I gave one last tweak in the rikono's mind at the point to open his awareness, and then Tybot opened his eyes.

'Are we going to meld or not?' he sent.

'Nope,' I replied, 'it's too dangerous,' the dog had absolutely no memory of what had transpired; I decided to keep it that way.

I walked up the stairs with Q'asha mentally replaying to her all that had happened; the Raybaros had precluded the Keeper, why neither Q'asha nor I could understand. Perhaps the urgency of the moment made it easier for only one of us to be linked quite so deeply to that massive mind.

I began again the following morning on the pile of papers, this time Tybot lay at my feet; I didn't want the rikono out of my sight. Not after the previous night's episode anyway.

ANAKIM

Luck was with him. At least, regarding Samlazaz, he hadn't heard. In other ways... Well.

Kokablel stomped away angrily from the clutch of his fellows who were making ready to adopt rock form, joining their Gurts in sleeping the hot, bright daylight hours away. He'd paced no more than a few hundred strides from the assembly before his senses began initiating a search. Catching a whiff, the trace of a tear, he stood and began waving his arms in the prescribed manner. At the third attempt he caught an edge. Reaching inside, Kokablel pulled it open and stepped through.

~

Holborn Circus
London, England.
September 2008.

A red object smashed into him. High as his knee, its impact almost knocked him from his feet. All around him were hollow rocks, hills, and mountains full of bright lights and tasty worms.

They scurried away from him. Fast, but not fast enough. How he would feast. He delighted in their taste.

The red rock began to spurt a warm, fluid over his foot. He rolled his head down his leg, to where his limb had been struck by the thing and licked, tasting. It was created from rocks, many different kinds of rock, but rocks all the same. Rocks and silicates that had been melted in fire and their shapes altered.

That interested him, but he hadn't time for study. Providing for the troop was of greater importance. One of the worms was hanging halfway through a broken slice of silicate at the front of the rolling rock. He pulled it free; it had been trapped amongst the crumpled and broken pieces. Wriggling, it made a screeching sound through a hole in its exposed end. He lifted it to his nose and sniffed. It smelt good. Kokablel bit off the exposed piece, crunching the crispy morsel, relishing the exquisite taste of the juices as they flowed across his tongue and around his mouth, ravishing his senses. He felt his blood race, his senses sparkle. He swallowed the delicious piece, sucked the remainder dry, and then threw the remnants away. It was too much trouble to peel off the inedible outer coverings.

All about him were rocks of various shapes and sizes. Hundreds of the worms moved about in them, issuing their high-pitched noises. The rolling rocks had come to a halt when the red one smashed into him; they too had worms inside. Some held one or two, but others, the larger red ones, were full.

A white rock, with flashing blue lights and emitting a howling noise, wove its way through the stationary rocks towards him. Its wailing was annoying. Wrenching his foot free he made his way towards it, kicking other stationery rocks out of his path. Upon reaching it Kokablel stamped on the wailing blue and white rock three times. Defenceless, it crumpled and flattened. Instantly, the annoying howls ceased.

The first rock that had crashed into him was packed with worms, most of them waving miniature arms and opening their holes to squeal as they attempted to escape from the two levels. Easily, Kokablel lifted it, swinging it smoothly onto his shoulder.

With his free hand he began picking up scattered worms which lay unmoving, across the ground. There were some he noticed massing, trying frantically to get back into a hole in the ground from where they had previously spewed in their hundreds. He snatched up handfuls of them, stuffing them into his cavernous pouch. Inside it many were still moving. Others that had fallen out of the red rock were still.

As soon as his pouch was loaded, he waved his free arm, feeling once again for the tear.

Finding it where he'd left it; Kokablel stepped through, allowing it to close behind him.

THE SOUTHERN PLAINS

Kokablel dropped the red rock and emptied his pouch next to it. Some of the worms were still moving, opening their holes and screeching. He picked them up, one after the other, and with a swift squeeze stopped both their wriggling and the annoying noise.

Araklba the cook should be pleased: there was more than enough food for one night. Good food, too, in Kokablel's opinion. True, they needed cleaning and stripping of their inedible outer coverings, but drying and salting should make them nice and crisp, although personally he preferred them fresh and raw.

'How come you got worms? I thought you'd have gone for the four legged-brownies with the sharp, pointed heads. Much more meat on them,' his commander, half in and out of 'rock form,' said, rolling forward, to investigate.

'Guess I got the wrong tear, sir.'

'Well, you can take that stupid red thing away. It's annoying my senses.'

'Yes, sir,' Kokablel acquiesced with a half-hearted salute.

He lifted the now empty rock onto his shoulder, and marched back to the tear tremor area.

'Get some decent meat while you're there. This lot won't last long. It's all dead, won't keep,' the patrol cook shouted after him.

Now Kokablel was annoyed. Not only did he have to get rid of the red rock which he liked, but that waster Araklba wanted more meat. When were they going to understand that the only meat they really needed was the worms?

At this rate, probably never.

At the first tear he found, Kokablel stepped through and with all his prodigious strength heaved the empty red rock. The region was another of those infested, mountainous areas. What damage the falling rock might wreak, he cared not. Without taking any notice of where it landed, he stepped back, closing the tear behind him.

Swiftly searching other nearby tears, he found one opening onto the habitat of thousands of the four-legged, pointy-headed brownies. Kokablel filled his pouch with the bawling creatures, once again taking time to gobble one for himself, as he picked up the others. He was disappointed that consuming it brought no marked increase of his powers. Only the worms did that. Only they made his blood sing.

It was sunset when he finally made his way back to camp, and his colleagues were slowly awakening. Darkness would fully descend before the Gurts stirred and they could move out. Plenty of time for a proper meal, then. Kokablel made for the cook fires to empty his pouch. Araklba laughed. 'Maybe you get tomorrow off, matie. Thanks for this little lot. Well done.'

'Bog off,' Kokablel snapped, removing his pouch and shaking it to make sure all the muck and rubbish was cleared out.

The London Evening Standard.
September 30th 2008.
STOP PRESS.
Stone Giant Rocks up mayhem at Busy City Crossroads.

75 dead, 140 missing.
Government in Confusion.
Holborn, London.

During the rush hour at 8:00AM this morning, commuters were attacked by a horrendous giant creature. The number 38 bus was crossing the junction of Tottenham Court Road and Euston Road, when it was in collision with a creature which appeared to be created from granite slabs.

The stone clad giant carrying a massive pouch, caused mayhem, smashing numerous vehicles, including a police car. Witnesses described the creature as a three to four storey nightmare, which lifted a Double-Decker bus onto its shoulder before disappearing with almost one hundred and forty people which it had packed into its pouch.

Experts examining the CCTV recordings of the incident have put its height at between eleven to twelve meters.

Police too are examining these CCTV images.

The Prime Minister has called for an immediate investigation and a Ministerial Report.

Pictures and eye-witness reports; on pages, 2, 3, 4 and 5.

The New York Times
September 30th 2020, 08:48EST
London Double-Decker Flies In.
New York. USA.

At 08:48 today, a London Double-Decker bus flew from the junction of West 64th Street, down Broadway before crashing into the base of the Columbus Circle monument, causing eighteen deaths and twenty seven serious injuries.

The bus has been identified as the same vehicle which disappeared from a crowded intersection in Holborn London, twelve years previously.

NYPD is currently in communication with Scotland Yard.

The Daily Nation.
10th April, 1957.
Nairobi, Kenya.

Reports are coming in to our offices of a number of sightings of giant, grey rock clad creatures, seen chasing and catching wildebeest near the Ngorongoro Crater. Local Masai tribesmen are saying they are servants of Engai, the mountain God, and are forecasting doom will follow soon.

These sightings have not been corroborated, and have been attributed to a spate of liqueur thefts in the nearby township of Arusha in Northern Tanzania.

DEATH OF A GIANT

'Stop! Go to the present day,' shouted Rob.

As soon as they had flipped through time, they both heard Williard's cry for help. Instantly they ported to the location the trooper had sent to Araes.

~

A massive creature was standing, waving its arms about as if trying to find something, the air around it sparkled and crackled with static electricity, or was it magic?

'Anakim' shouted Rob, recognising the creature the Watcher had described. 'Take out its eyes.' Aiusha materialised in front of it and with a mighty roar blasted a stream of super-hot fire directly into the giant's face. The Anakim gave a horrendous scream and blindly flailed its arms trying to swat the dragon. Aiusha blasted it again. The creature raised its hands to its face to protect against further damage.

Rob leapt onto the giant's shoulder; looking down at the three amazed troopers he sent a powerful command, 'HAMSTRING IT, SLASH ITS ANKLE TENDONS!' Without a thought for their own safety the three youngsters leapt onto their runners and raced towards the giant creature, swords flying into their hands.

Pulling at a slab of rock with his superhuman strength, Rob managed to expose a piece of flesh at the back of the creature's head. Aiusha blasted yet another fumarole onto the giant's hands, causing it to scream once again. At that moment Rob thrust his spear deep into the Anakim's brain, following it with a blast of fire from his right hand and a spear of ice from his left, both exploding deep within, at the tip of his weapon. The giant rocked but still managed to hold its position. Looking down from where he floated suspended behind the creature's head, he could see the troopers struggling to remove the armour rocks from the giant's ankles. Swooping down, Rob joined their efforts, the four of them assisted by the Runners managed to expose both ankles.

Pulling his sword from behind his back Rob hacked at one mighty tendon, on the third blow he severed it, the creature took a step and stumbled, the troopers were attacking the other ankle in like manner, it gave way to their onslaught. The Anakim fell to one knee, Rob and his little team scampered aside as the giant began its slow fall forwards. With a mighty crash it landed face down and began to groan loudly. Aiusha alighted at the hole Rob had created at the back of its head, as Rob ran across the giant's body to join her. Removing his bloody spear, he stabbed again, deeper this time. Rob drove another ice spear into the creature, The Purple Queen with a murmured warning, blasted in concert with Rob, a torrent of ice spears and flames were driven into its brain, once again exploding at the tip of Rob's spear.

The sensation of static electricity ceased, all was quiet.

'It's dead,' proclaimed Rob, jumping to the ground and high fiving the trio of troopers.

'What the fuck is it?' asked Williard,

'Anakim,' sent Rob and the lion headed trooper together.

~

There was a commotion from the huge sack the creature had been carrying. Turning their attention to it, the troopers, the runners and the Purple Queen all gasped to see strangely garbed injured and blood covered humans beginning to crawl from within.

REUNION

A Blue materialised with a crash in the sky above us, even before it landed, my two girls leapt from its back and rushed towards me with cries of joy. We collapsed on the ground in a happy tussle of gold, black and purple bodies much to the amusement of the troopers and the Purple Queen. I noticed they were both slim and fit, 'Are the babies alright?' I asked with trepidation in my thoughts. I was met with a flood of joyous thoughts, 'They are at the caves, you will see them soon beloved,' replied Keysha.

'I'm sad I missed their births,' I said, my arms around them both, tears in my eyes. Toana wiped my eyes, and nuzzled her face to mine.

'You didn't miss much, just a couple of screaming females squeezing their birthing muscles,' Keysha yipped her cute little laugh.

~

But a more crucial problem was raising its head, how to deal with the traumatised humans, that were still exiting the massive red sack.

Williard and Carilla

THE HUMANS

There was a whole heap of weeping, wailing and screaming from the fifty living, walking wounded humans who scrambled from the sack.

Confused, we stood stunned considering what we could do to help.

Out of the clear blue sky, appeared the giant Red, Lord Dominie. He landed beside us and stood for a moment surveying the scene. The humans were overcome and many fainted or fell to the ground shaking in fear at the sight of him

'WHAT TO DO, FATHER?' queried Aiusha.

'I HAVE A PLAN, IT MIGHT WORK, BUT I NEED YOU FIVE TO COME WITH ME,' the three troopers sank to the ground, when the adrenalin from the battle wore off, replaced with reverence as the Red appeared.

The human survivors were now attempting to crawl back inside the sack in utter panic. Three dragons, one; the red, standing taller than a house. The blue and the purple half its size. A purple clad man who appeared to be their leader, two lion headed and two dog headed creatures, a short young man with olive skin, all carrying vicious looking swords, spears and crossbows, and lastly three fierce looking giant lizards, was too much, all that, along with the sight of a mountain of rocks and flesh that had recently been their captor, was enough to send them scuttling back into the sack, despite it being already occupied by over a hundred injured or deceased fellow captives.

Lord Dominie waddled to the handles of the sack, grasped them with one front foot and said to his companions, 'MOUNT UP AND FOLLOW ME.'

The two other dragons with their riders disappeared with the giant red.

FORT BRIMAT

The group materialised over Fort Brimat and carefully landed in the open centre circle. It was coming on dusk, and the townsfolk were preparing for their evening meal. The commotion was enough to bring them rushing from their homes. Lord Dominie, Aiusha and the Blue; Crostamos, assumed miniaturised versions of themselves, standing eye to eye with me.

A crowd gathered around us, the air was full of questioning mind speech; the two girls and I slammed up our barriers before we were overwhelmed. 'KEEP STILL AND WAIT,' sent the red in a powerful broadcast. The crowd watching sank to one knee, their heads bowed, obviously in veneration of the three M'ntar.

Stepping through the kneeling people walked a tall woman accompanied by a young blonde haired maiden. They both bowed deeply to the three dragons, who acknowledged them with a nod of their heads.

'Q'ASHA AND Q'REM, AND ALL YOU PEOPLE OF FORT BRIMAT, I HAVE A TASK I WOULD REQUEST OF YOU, INSIDE THIS SACK ARE A NUMBER OF HUMANS WHO HAVE BEEN BADLY INJURED AND TERRIFIED BY THE ANAKIM, OUR MORTAL ENEMIES, I ASK THAT YOU TAKE CARE OF THEM ON OUR BEHALF. I LEAVE THREE OF MY DEAREST FRIENDS WITH YOU TO ASSIST. DO YOU ACCEPT THIS TASK AS A GIFT TO ME?

'Certainly Lord,' replied the Q'rem, echoed moments later by a loud mental shout of acceptance from the entire population.

I was momentarily taken aback, for I recognised the mental voice of the teenager; she was the mysterious mind I had perceived, when I was first in the M'ntar caves at last a puzzle had been answered.

'MY KIN AND I ARE RETURNING TO OUR HOME, WE HAVE MUCH TO DISCUSS WITH OUR CLAN, BUT WE SHALL RETURN IMMEDIATELY SHOULD YOU REQUIRE US, TAKE HEED OF WHAT ROB SAYS, FOR HE IS THE COMPANION AND RIDER OF THE PURPLE QUEEN, HE IS M'NTAR IN ALL BUT BODY.'

~

With that the three M'ntar leapt into the air, with an outwards rush of wind as the air was pushed away from their giant bodies assuming full size, and followed by a thunderous crack of inrushing air as they disappeared.

Quickly recovering, the townsfolk nearest to the sack opened it wide exposing the petrified inhabitants inside. With soft coaxing words they enticed the walking out. Others entered the bloody sack and brought out those injured or unable to walk, they were all taken away to individual home-domes to be helped and tended to, overseen by the tall woman and her blonde assistant.

The dead were left inside the sack, to be disposed of in the unique method employed by the locals. As dark was beginning to fall, no one was prepared to venture outside the walls. From the minds of some of the townsfolk nearest to us we gleaned information about the Ragies, or Killers as the Mustique called them.

Once all the living had been moved to where they could be helped and attended to, the two girls and I, who had received many a querulous look whilst we helped extract the badly injured, at my suggestion we kept our minds closed. Q'asha, the tall woman who seemed to be the settlement leader approached us.

'Ta 't ee for y'r assist,' she said in a strange version of English, which had it not been for my mind reading ability, I would have found difficult to understand. I replied in mind speech. Momentarily she was taken aback but replied, 'We welcome you to our township, would you come with me, I am happy to offer you my home and a meal. Plus I am so intrigued to know all about you, how you look as you do, where are you from, and how you came to be riders of the Raybaros.' That I understood was their name for their revered M'ntar.

'Thank you,' we three replied in concert. I could foresee that a considerable length of time was going to be spent asking and answering questions from both sides.

ROB AND Q'ASHA

An hour later the walking wounded, and those lucky few who had come through the horrifying experience without harm, some eighty-four souls in all, assembled in the inner quadrangle of Fort Brimat. I stood on a raised box, The towns folk had arranged a small dais and the area was lit by lights from open doors of the surrounding home-domes. Behind me stood the inhabitants of Brimat, minds open.

The bodies of the dead and the huge bag had been removed.

~

I began, speaking in the ancient language English, which the majority of the captives were speaking, amongst themselves.

'My name is Captain Robert Clitheroe-Winthorpe, of the subterranean city of Castra, rider of my companion The Purple Queen. These are my pledges Toana daughter of the Tirnano Clan, and Keysha child of the Brosynan Tribe, I would like to introduce you to Lady Q'asha, Leader and Healer of the people of Fort Brimat.

'From my deductions, and listening to you speak, you have come from a land known as England, the year when you left was 1980. I don't know how to break this to you gently but that was more than five thousand years in the past, this is your future.

A clamour of questions was fired at me as I paused to take a sip of water and collect my thoughts. 'I'll answer as many of your concerns as I can when I have finished,' I said flatly.

'Who do you think you are, we don't have to take orders from you?' A thick set middle aged man shouted angrily, and scrambled to his feet.

'And who are you?' I asked coldly.

'Henry Swift, I am a member of Parliament, The Minister for Agriculture.' He replied pompously.

'Well Mr. Swift, I have two things to say to you: One, if it was not for the intervention of these two young ladies, three of my mounted troopers, our M'ntar colleagues and myself, you probably would have been stirring gently in a rather large stew pot by now, if you hadn't been eaten raw as a starter.

'And two, it might interest you to know that here, in this place until such time as you become experienced if you don't do as I, or any of these people behind me, trained and experienced fighters says; instantly and without argument, you will die. We do not play games here, this is a battlefield and you have arrived in the midst of a war. Now do you wish to ask me any more questions, or make any more comments? Please save it to the end, because I would like to continue?'

Henry Swift MP gave a shocked grunt and sat down almost as quickly as he had stood. A few of the survivors clapped, one shouted, 'You tell him mister!' The others simply sat with fear and trepidation written on their faces.

'You fizzin' overly much sweet cheeks, I'll handle this for a bit.' - 'Any of you medically trained?' asked Q'asha, picking up Rob's annoyed thoughts and taking over. Toana sniggered, having followed the mental interchange. 'We need medics of any kind.' Q'asha said.

'Aren't you going to let us go home?' It was Henry Swift again.

'Mr. Swift,' I interjected, 'If it was possible to be able to return you to the time and place of your departure, more than five thousand years ago, I would be pleased to do so right now, and with a size nine to assist, - but until such time as a lot of clever minds can give their full attention to the matter, for at the moment we are battling to keep the golem from encroaching into this part of our world, you and anyone else who feels they have priority will have to wait.'

'How long?' Swift was determined to have his say.

'As long as it takes. - I think I posed a question.' Q'asha's voice was flat as she fought down the desire to join Rob and administer a kick in the politician's butt.

Out of the eighty-four now sat in front of us, for others festooned in bandages had joined. Fifteen raised their hands; one was the woman who had initially spoken to Rob.

'That's a good percentage,' sent Q'asha.

'We are a group from St. Bart's, off duty and on a day out. Didn't expect to come quite this far though,' said the woman with an embarrassed giggle.

'Can you come and join us for a moment,' I gestured to her. The woman rose to her feet and weaved her way through the seated group.

'How many can be opened?' I sent to the two girls.

'OF THE ENTIRE GROUP, SOME FIFTY-SEVEN WOULD BE COMFORTABLE, FOUR WOULD STRUGGLE FOR A WHILE TO ASSIMILATE, AND THE REMAINDER WOULD NOT BE SUITABLE.' Toana responded to me. 'THE FAT ONE IS NOT ONE OF THEM.'

I laughed out loud, startling the woman, who had arrived. 'Sorry, personal joke,' I said, reaching out to touch her shoulder reassuringly. 'What's your name?'

'Rona, Rona Cooper, I'm a ward sister.'

'Pleased to meet you Rona, sorry about the circumstances, we've only one medic, Lady Q'asha here, she'll be more than pleased to see you all, especially as we have some serious injuries amongst your colleagues.'

'But how, - I can't speak for the others, I need to get my head around this before I can say if I can help you.'

'Did you hear what Q'asha said to the politician?' Rob cut in.

'Um, yes, but...'

Rob turned to the group once more; he broadcast his anger with his mind as well as his voice... 'I have said once, and I am only going to repeat it this one time more, we are under a war footing here. You have been given a chance at life, where your life was about to be taken from you, you are still alive, be at least grateful.'

Q'asha took over again, 'In this place I am in command, what I say goes, you may not like it, and to be truthful I don't care. You are under military law, my law. I am not a petty despot, a dictator or whatever you deem to think of me. My motives are in order to keep you alive, nothing more and nothing less. I don't care if you hate my guts, but you will do as I, and my people say, or I will slap you in jail, and there you will stay until this is all over, or a giant decides you might look good on the end of a toasting fork, or one of our many noisy neighbours, who you can now hear, would like you for supper.'

Swift climbed to his feet, and began to speak, 'And you Mr. Swift, will be the first if you raise any more objections.'

'I had no intention of raising any objections, having heard what the two of you have said, I support you wholeheartedly madam, and if there is anything I can do please let me know.'

'We will Mr. Swift, we will,' said Rob 'Rona, I need your decision now, you and everyone else here,' Rob turned to the group, 'You either agree wholeheartedly to assist and integrate in any way possible, and as required, or you will be kept apart from everyone else until we are able, if ever, to return to your time. And yes, you heard right, I said 'if ever.' - If you are prepared to join this expedition, then stand up now. I'm sorry if this sounds harsh, but you have ended up in a harsh world,'

Three teenagers, two boys and a girl remained seated; they were immediately escorted by two large sodjers away from the others.

Toana then singled out those the girls had targeted for opening, the three teenagers who had left the scene were amongst those eligible, Rob expressed his disappointment to Q'asha, who mentally shrugged, 'that's the way it goes.'

FROZEN

Frozen in a grotesque parody of flight, its wings still and mute, the moth hung a hair's breadth from the bizarre, motionless candle flame, transfixed a heartbeat from an incandescent death. A voice in her mind screamed again, demanding attention, clawing at her sanity, shredding the final remnants of her sleep. She sat upright, her body shaking. The cot saturated with her sweat shook as she swung her legs to the floor.

Fear manifested itself in an impromptu dribble that made its way down her inner thigh. Making her feet she picked up and pulled on the night-shirt that had slipped to the floor. On trembling legs she crossed to the dresser and without bothering to use a nearby mug, gulped several mouthfuls from the oodooce bottle. Fortified, she climbed the stairs stepped to the opening and stepped out into the morning mist. Her mind shuddered in complaint.

Of the many fushmen, sodjers and kitchiedeems who would normally be preparing for the day, some sodjers with bowls in hand, waiting to be fed after their shift. Soup from ladles hung in the air like thick brown rope. All were as wax figurines on display, part of some sick macabre joke. But it wasn't a joke. like the candle in her tent, the fires that normally lit the harbour, glowing brightly, but now did not flicker, nor give off heat or light. The silence and stillness did nothing to allay the mounting red mist of panic that rose in her breast.

Her senses became aware of movement, in this place of sculptures, she spun to her left. A lioness headed female - tall, more than twice her height, and dressed in a revealing two piece in red and white - strode towards her. At her side, padded the largest Black Panther Q'rem had ever seen. She imagined in a ridiculous moment how small her head would look in that cavernous mouth, and shuddered. But, neither black cat nor the lioness headed creature frightened her as much as the hooked sickle the giant carried.

Almost flat, it permeated an odour of death, and harboured a power she could feel clamouring at her mind. Something was trapped within that blade, something that was screaming for release.

'I am Sekhmet, you will come with me,' commanded the goddess.

Unable to resist, Q'rem followed, she strode through an open field, where was the settlement? It had disappeared...

~

'What is this?' She asked, as she struggled to keep pace with the fifteen foot tall warrior. 'Am I dreaming?'

'This is no dream such as you would understand, you have been summoned, you are the one touched by Isis, and Ra would meet with you.'

'But what of my parents, my dog, I should leave them knowledge of this.'

'It is forbidden,' came a flat toned reply. Q'rem knew immediately the subject was closed.

Unable to believe she was not embroiled in some strange interactive dream, Q'rem followed, but was unable to stop herself from blurting 'But what am I to do with all this, and where are we going?'

At that moment they came to the banks of a wide river, a boat waited there, the waves lapping gently against its side. 'Get in,' commanded the goddess.

Confused, Q'rem as she was bid, climbed aboard and sat in the bow facing the middle, where Sekhemt and the Black Panther took their places. High in the stern stood a normal sized man. With a pole he pushed the barque away from the shore and out into the dark water. In the milky early morning light Q'rem could make out a far bank.

SEKHEMET

The goddess began to speak into her mind.

'You would perceive all to be as it is, if I relate to you the story of The Blood of Isis.

~

'Geb and Nut had issue of two sets of twins.

'Of the four, Osiris was a wise lord who brought to you, Amun-Ra's cattle civilization. He taught you savages, who previously delighted in eating of each other, and the offal of unclean creatures, to cultivate the rich banks of Mother River. He gave to you the art of living in peace and harmony. He taught you the joy of worshiping the great ones and showed how they responded by granting untold blessings. You were joyful to be of service to the lords who came from afar to live amongst you.

'But Seth the chaos Lord was envious of his brother Osiris, and the peaceful worship he received, for Seth craved war, death and destruction. He conceived a plan in which he tricked Osiris to lie in a beautiful, carved and ornate box. Seth then closed the lid and sealed it, making it into a coffin. He threw the coffin into mother Nile so it would drift away. Isis searched for the coffin, when she found it she hid it in a swamp. Once more Seth heard of it and went hunting for the body. In a fit of anger he took the body of his brother, dismembered it and threw the pieces to all corners of the earth.

'Isis through the use of her magic searched for the lost pieces of her brother-husband. The King of Byblos offered the protection of his home and the help of his empire in recovering Osiris body, but Isis in her anguish and her ruthless resolve, her mind full of contradictions killed two of his sons, horrifying repayment for his friendship. However with the assistance of her sister Nephthys they found and reassembled Osiris, Isis breathed life into his dead body, then she lay with him and conceived a son, Horus.'

Seth though constantly searched for the child, intent upon his death. Many were the dangers that faced Horus after birth, and Isis fled far with the newborn to escape his wrath, for the murderer of her husband would not rest until he had his will. Isis and Nephthys protected and raised Horus until he was old enough to face Seth.

'Horus took terrible vengeance upon Seth for his father's murder in a mighty battle in which Seth struck out the eye of Horus, Horus in return castrated his uncle. Geb in an effort to stop the battle before one or the other were slain, separated the combatants giving them domain over opposite ends of the sky.

'Nephthys had been forbidden to have a child by Seth, and following his castration, had disguised herself as the more beautiful Isis and danced before Osiris, Inflamed with lust and passion he lay with her and the result of that union was a son, Anubis.

Osiris with his intimate knowledge of death, now lived as the god of the dead, the ruler of the underworld.

'Because Seth would have slain the young Anubis if he knew he were his wife's son, Nephthys convinced Isis to raise the boy as her own.'

'That's seriously interesting, but what has it to do with me, and why am I having this crazy dream?' Q'rem asked, still unable to believe that she could not be dreaming, and yet if she were, how could she be aware that it was but a dream?

The barque came in close to land at that point; Q'rem could make out buildings in the distance.

'Listen, that I may conclude before you face Osiris, lest you be found ignorant in his eyes. --- So it was when you humans had become acceptable to them, the children of Atum found the daughters of men to be attractive, and took them to themselves as concubines, and those concubines yet bore children who in turn joined the gods and became as giants among men.'

'So if this god Osiris is the god of the dead, why am I meeting him?' asked Q'rem.

'So that you may understand the task that you and I have been chosen to perform,' replied the lioness headed giant.

'The four have split,' she continued, 'the Great Ennead of Heliopolis no longer contrive as one. The reasons for their dissension with Ra were many, but have been resolved. Seth alone is not placated, he blames the ancient peoples of your world for his emasculation, and his revenge is to be the ruination of your world, that world from which you came. To this end he brings death from the deepest depths of the heavens, not for the first time he has hurled death and destruction at you Ra's cattle.'

'Why should he blame us?'

'Your ancients worshiped Osiris, elevating him to be the greatest of the gods under Ra, giving him their reverence, sacrifices and supplications. This caused the god of death and re-birth to have greatness and power surpassing all others. Osiris brought life, in the form of agriculture, to all living humans. Incarnate in their pharaohs, Osiris created life for the living in the administration of the state. As the lord of the dead, Osiris represented the moral order of the universe, judging each soul by its life and rewarding or punishing that soul with a rigorous justice.

'Seth was vilified as Osiris' murderer and his standing vastly reduced this he could not countenance, and vowed his revenge upon mankind for the error of their ways.'

'What about the other Gods, can't they stop him?'

'Not alone. That which he began so long ago, must be allowed to play to its conclusion, only then may he be brought to task for his deeds.'

'That doesn't seem fair, the destruction of the human race first, then he is guilty?'

'As yet it has not come to pass; until it has he has no guilt. Mankind has caused the gods to grow weak and feeble through their lack of worship.'

'What do you mean by that?'

'No longer do Ra's cattle give worship, no longer do the great ones receive sacrifice and prayer, for the world of your past became a godless world, only wars and chaos reigned supreme in their hearts. The balance had been lost. The God of Chaos holds sway over all except Ra, only Ra retains supreme power, for some yet still give praise for each day's dawning, worshiping the sun, but even that weakens.'

'I've done a wee bittie o' that, grabbing a quick bronzy in ma time,' remarked Q'rem absently.

The barque came to rest gently against the bank. Ahead Q'rem could see columns and buildings stretching to the horizon on either side.

'Sheesh this dream is getting crazier by the minute, wait'll I tell Q'asha, she's daft enough to figure it out.'

People her own size appeared all around, prostrating themselves before the giant goddess who clicked her tongue once against her teeth, the humans rose from the dust almost as one and formed an escort. The huge Black Panther preceded the pair as they made their way side by side towards a covered veranda.

'STOP HERE, LORD OSIRIS APPROACHES.' Sekhemt commanded, and dropped to one knee, raising her hands before her face, her palms forward. The escorts assumed a face down position, prostrate once again. A sharp hiss from the panther sent

Q'rem swiftly to her knees; she lowered her head and assumed the same position as the lioness headed goddess.

OSIRIS

A deep croaking voice began to intone; 'I am the only being in an abyss of Darkness. From an abyss of Darkness came I forth ere my birth, from the silence of a primal sleep. And the voice of ages said unto my soul, 'I am he who formulates in Darkness, the Light that shineth in the Darkness, yet the Darkness comprehendeth it not.' Let the mystical circumambulation take place onto the Path of Darkness that leadeth unto Light with the Lamp of Hidden Knowledge to guide the way.'

ISIS

At this point a beautiful woman, almost as tall as Sekhemt stepped forward, she knelt in homage before Osiris. She began to sing; 'Hail to thee, Osiris, lord of eternity, king of the gods, thou who hast many names, thou disposer of created things, thou who hast hidden forms in the temples, thou sacred one, thou KA who dwellest in all the diverse worlds; Thou who gavest life to this child, offspring of another world, thou who will annointest with honey the lips of this child that her words will drip sweetness, her eyes you will bathe with the clear waters of the land of many rivers that her sight be sure and pure. Thou shall annointest her forehead with oil pressed from the fruit of the olive bush, that she may consider all things with power and knowledge.

To her will be obedient the stars in the heights, thou shall openest the mighty gates for her that she may pass between the worlds thereof with freedom of step. She will be the leader to whom hymns of praise are sung in the southern heaven, and unto her will adorations be paid in the northern heavens. The never setting stars are before her face, and they are her thrones, even as also are those that never rest. An offering cometh to her by the command of Seb. The company of the gods adoreth her, the stars of the Tuat bow to the earth in adoration before her, All domains pay homage to her, and the ends of the earth will offer entreaty and supplication.

'When those who are among the fallen ones see this child they will tremble before her, and the whole world giveth praise unto her when it meeteth her majesty.

'To her they will cry - 'Thou art a glorious sahu among the sahu's, upon thee hath dignity been conferred, thy dominion is eternal.'

Another goddess, almost as striking as the first stepped forward and prostrated herself before Osiris. At his command Nephthys rose to her knees, extended her wings and began to worship him.

NEPHTHYS

'My brother Osiris, firstborn son of the womb of Nut, begotten of Seb, the prince of gods and men, the god of gods, the king of kings, the lord of lords, the prince of princes, the governor of the world, from the womb of Nut, whose existence is the everlasting soul that liveth again, the being who becometh a child again, the firstborn son of unformed matter, the lord of multitudes of aspects and forms, the lord of time and the bestower of years, the lord of life for all eternity. Yours is the 'giver of life from the beginning;' life springs up to you from its destruction, and the germ which proceeds from her, engenders life in both the dead and the living.'

SEKHMET EXPLAINS

It was a short while after the vista had played out and the entourage of Osiris had departed. Q'rem sat on a huge couch whilst Sekhmet reclined upon a bed; the Lioness seemed fretful, her eyes flicking around the room as if searching for signs of a hidden intruder.

'Tell me of those gods, Seth and Horus, what is it about them that can cause such a current of hatred, the air itself crackles with fury?'

The goddess looked towards her charge and gave a sigh.

THE NEVER ENDING WARS

'It is said that the great battles between Horus and Seth first began during the three hundred and sixty-third year of the reign of Ra-Herakhty on Earth and ended many decades later. Ra had assembled a massive army in Nubia in preparation for an attack on Seth who had rebelled against him. From a boat floating on the river he directed his troops of footmen, horsemen, and archers. Among them was Horus who had long sought to avenge his father's death but had been unable to trap Seth in battle.

'Horus, who loved an hour of fighting more than a day of feasting, looked forward to the battle with glee. Thoth gave the young god magical powers to transform himself into a solar disk with large golden wings the colour of the sky at sunset; in this form young Horus led Ra's troops into battle and prepared his tactics for their first encounter.

'When Horus sighted the legions of Seth, he rose on his great wings above them and uttered a curse: 'Your eyes shall be blinded and you shall not see; your ears shall be deaf and you shall not hear.' The enemy beneath him suddenly became confused: each warrior looked at the soldier next to him, and deceived by the power of the curse, saw a stranger where moments before an ally had stood. The speech around him sounded like a foreign language. The warriors cried out that their ranks had been infiltrated by the enemy, and they turned and fell upon each other.

In a moment the army had defeated itself.

'Meanwhile, Horus was hovering above, looking for Seth. His archenemy stood not in this advance guard, but had hidden in the marshes to the north.

'Horus continued to have trouble cornering Seth in battle, even though he was to chase Seth's troops through three more battles in the south and six in the north. Some took place in rivers, where the combatants changed themselves into crocodiles and hippopotamuses, some took place on land where again the slaughter of warriors was terrible, and one was even fought on the high seas between the stars.

'On one occasion when Horus thought he had captured his chief enemy during the heat of a battle, he cut off the soldier's head and severed the body into fourteen pieces as Seth had cut up Osiris. Once the dust from the battle had settled, however, Horus finally saw his victim clearly and realized he had been fooled once again; the wrong enemy had fallen into his hands, merely a simulacrum of the Chaos Lord.

Seth had escaped him once again.'

~

'Years later, when Horus had matured, Seth challenged him to single handed combat. Isis decorated her son's boat with gold and prayed for his success. Seth took the form of a red hippopotamus and prepared for battle on the Island of Elephants. With a great voice like thunder he used his power over storms as a terrible weapon. The waves and wind tossed Horus' boats about, but the young god stood fast in the prow and led his followers through the worst of the storm. At the point of blackest darkness, the foam of the waters made the golden boat shine like the rays of the sun.

'As the storms lessened, the two gods began their long-due battle, which is said to have lasted three hundred years. Somehow during the confusion Seth wrested Horus' left eye from his head, no doubt because he disguised himself as a black pig, and tricked Horus into letting him close. Horus redoubled his efforts and recaptured his eye, which later he was to feed to Osiris to ensure his eternal life. Horus revenged himself upon Seth for this injury by seizing the red god, ripping off his testicles.

'At one point in the fighting Horus gained the upper hand and tied up his adversary. He asked Isis to guard Seth while he went in pursuit of the enemy army, but Seth tricked Isis with sweet words about her duty to her brother. Finally, Isis felt so guilty she loosened Seth's ropes and allowed him to escape. When Horus discovered what had been done, he was so outraged that he cut his mother's head from her body with one blow of his knife. Fortunately Thoth was nearby and quickly replaced her missing head along with the horns and solar disk of Hathor.

With Seth at large again, Horus had to return to battle. The young god eight cubits tall, held a harpoon with a blade measuring four cubits. He handled this mighty weapon as if it weighed no more than a reed. This time, when he sighted his long-time foe, he aimed with all his skill. The first cast caught the red hippopotamus full in the head and entered his brain, Seth refused to admit defeat and fled to his mountain home.

The conflict was finally brought before the senior gods who assembled at Heliopolis as a court, to hear the plea of young Horus against his uncle Seth. Atum-Ra sat in the chair as chief judge and Thoth was the main spokesman for the young god. The dilemma before the court was whether Horus should receive Osiris' position on earth because he was blood heir, or whether Seth should receive it because he was older and still fit to rule. Shu and others argued: 'Justice should prevail over sheer strength. Deliver judgment saying 'Give the office to Horus.'

But Atum-Ra was not happy. Fearing Seth's warlike character and knowing that his retaliation if the case went against him would be more troublesome than anything Horus could attempt. He wanted to appease the red haired god and was angry with the court for giving in to Horus so easily. Seth then proposed that he and Horus resolve the issue through trial by combat, but Thoth asked the court if it would not be better to try to find out who was right and who was wrong rather than leaving the decision to a fight.

When Osiris asked if there were some approach other than combat, the gods decided that they were trying to settle the case with insufficient information, and that they would write to Neith, the ancient goddess, renowned for her wisdom and request her guidance. At once Thoth, as secretary of the gods, composed a letter that concluded: 'What are we to do about these two fellows who have now been before the court for eight hundred years without our being able to decide between them? Please write and tell us what to do.' Neith replied that the court should give Osiris' position to Horus, and mollify Seth by offering him a couple of minor goddesses to dally with.

The court was pleased with this compromise and immediately decided Neith had great wisdom.

When Atum-Ra still refused to agree with the court, the other gods grew increasingly angry with him. Over the uproar, one god screamed at Atum-Ra:

'Your shrine is empty!' Such an insult, of course, could not pass unnoticed, and Atum-Ra went sulking back to his house where he lay on his back without talking to anyone. Hathor, his daughter saw that something had to be done for the old god, and decided to tease him out of his ill humour. She danced in front of him whipped up her gown, and bared her private parts before his startled eyes. Atum-Ra laughed out loud and returned to court in a better frame of mind.

He commanded the opponents to debate the matter in open court, where Seth and Horus repeated their old arguments. When the court agreed with Seth, Isis became angry and the court assured her that Horus would win the position. Seth, furious with his sister, told Atum-Ra that he would have nothing more to do with the court as long as Isis was around to influence it. Atum-Ra decided that a change in venue was in order and moved the court to another world. The ferryman, Anty, was ordered not to take Isis or anyone who looked like her across the heavenly waters.

Isis, plotting to join the others on the world, disguised herself as an old woman with a bent back. Carrying a jar of barley and wearing a gold ring, she approached Anty and asked for a ride: 'I have come for you to ferry me to Middle Island. I am taking a jar of barley to my little boy tending cattle there; he has been there five days and will be getting hungry.' Anty protested that he was not supposed to ferry women, but she asked if his orders were not for Isis alone. Succumbing to temptation and believing it safe to help this old woman, he asked what she would give him if he consented. She offered some barley, but he refused, declaring that he would not violate his orders for some bread. She then offered the ring, and to no one's surprise he took it.

Once on the world, she turned herself into a beautiful, seductive maiden. When Seth saw her, he left the court and called out from behind a bush, 'I would like to tarry here with you, fair child.'

Coyly she set her trap: 'Ah, my great lord! I was married to a shepherd and bore him a son, but my husband died and the boy had to look after his father's animals. Then a stranger came and hid in the barn and told my son: 'I will beat you, take away your father's animals, and chase you away.' May I persuade you to help my son?'

Seth, never known for his subtlety, and lusting after this fair creature, replied: 'Indeed, never should one give animals to a stranger while the man's son is at hand'

Isis immediately turned herself into a vulture and taunted her adversary from the branch of a tree: 'Bewail yourself! Your own mouth has said it and your own judgment has judged you!' When Seth returned to court, even Atum-Ra had to agree that Seth had been tricked into foolishly judging himself. Anty nevertheless was sent for, and the court ordered that his lower legs be cut off as punishment; rumour tells that he 'forswore the use of gold until this present day.'

When the court appeared ready to award the position to Horus, Seth challenged his nephew to yet another contest. This time they were to change themselves into hippopotami and dive into the sea. Whoever held his breath under water for three months would be the winner. After the two gods had dived under, Isis, fearing that Horus would lose, decided to help him. Taking an ingot of bronze she forged it into the head of a harpoon to which she fitted a long shaft, making a fearful weapon. Then she took careful aim at Seth in the water and threw the harpoon with all her divine strength. The weapon flew straight to and pierced the sacred body of Horus.

'With a cry of pain, he called his mother to remove the harpoon from his body. Regretting her mistake at once she used her magic to free the harpoon and then cast it once more at Seth and successfully held him fast. Seth in turn protested his treatment on the grounds that they too were flesh and blood. Moved by her brother's plea, Isis ordered the harpoon to release him.

'Following this event there seems to have been a truce declared, and Horus and Seth went off to try to resolve the problem themselves. Actually this was another of Seth's tricks, for as soon as he was alone with the young god he raped him, in the hope that once the other gods believed Horus was homosexual (only the recipient of the seed was deemed homosexual), they would repudiate him. Horus ran to his mother for help. She took some of his semen and dropped it on some lettuce, a symbol of sexual potency.

'When Seth unwittingly ate the seed of Horus in a salad, he became pregnant by his nephew. Soon he went to the court with his charge of homosexuality, and the court at first laughed at Horus for his supposed weakness. He denied the charges and challenged the court to call up his seed. When summoned, the seed inside Seth grew into a large disk on his head, but before he could remove it, Thoth grasped it and placed it on his own head as a headpiece. So the court sided with Horus.

'As usual when he was about to lose the decision, Seth again challenged Horus to combat. This time he suggested a race in boats made of stone. Horus readily agreed; he made a boat of cedar covered with gypsum to give it the appearance of stone, and set it floating on the water. Seth saw that his nephew had successfully launched what appeared to be a stone boat and hurried about doing the same. He cut the peak off a mountain and used the stone to build a large boat. He launched it and watched as it promptly and surely sank to the bottom.

'When the court intervened again and was about to award the position to Seth, who claimed victory by virtue of his nephew's deceit, Osiris, finally made a plea on his son's behalf. This brought him into argument with Atum-Ra, but despite the chief god's words, and threats from Seth, the court changed its mind once again and decided in favour of Horus. Again Seth challenged Horus to combat, but by now even the court had had enough.

'Isis now brought Seth into court bound in chains like a criminal. Atum-Ra asked him why he was not willing to allow the court to settle the case after eight hundred years. Much to everyone's surprise, Seth agreed to end the fighting and permitted Horus to accept the position of Osiris awarded by the court. Brought before the court and placed on the throne of his father with Osiris' own crown, Horus was told that he was the master of every world for all eternity.

'Ptah realized that justice was being done, but he saw that Seth was being deprived of power that some still believed he deserved. 'What shall be done with Seth?' he asked Atum-

Ra quickly realized that he could make use of Seth's warlike nature and ordered Seth to stay beside him like a son: 'He shall raise his voice in the sky and all shall be afraid of him.'

'Thus Seth was given a permanent place in the solar boat, as the god of storms. There he intimidated all beings and protected Atum-Ra from his enemies.'

RA

Gathering of the gods

The dawn, breaking across the sky brought relief, hope sprung in his breast. Will today be the day? Will today be different? He wondered.

Ra stepped from the night barque to the solar barque. Leaving the barque Mandet behind, he absorbed the pulsing of rejuvenation that flowed through his body. But eons were enough to have left their mark, never again would he know the spring of youth; the night journey through space and time has been cold, as it always was.

Aker raised his fist to his chest in a salute, 'Until this evening, Lord Ra.' He turned away, his leonine mane catching the first warm breeze of dawn, flowing around his face.

'Until then,' Replied Ra.

The solar barque Meseket, with Ma'at at its helm set sail, a new journey, the day has begun.

Ma'at gave her father a greeting, her face grave but behind her eyes flickered her dry sense of humour, revealed only in the moments when her guard was lowered. Her constant companion Ammut squats at her heels, his tongue lolling, his eyes observing all.

Ra moves towards the bow, he finds Bastet; she raises her head, stretches languorously and blinks a greeting. His love for this daughter is well known; of all his family she has never caused him grief. He strokes her head, the cat-goddess purrs loudly.

Seth is next to greet him, preening himself, flexing his powerful muscles, limbering up for the day ahead. He glances at his great-great-uncle; the wind blows a lock of his startling red hair into his eyes, without a greeting he returns to his exercises.

The Solar barque, the boat of a million years, leaves the eastern gate of heaven, the river of day runs smoothly, God of the waters Nun, guides the barque gently on its way.

Ra has hesitated by Seth, hesitated long enough that the Chaos Lord must raise his head. Seth's blood red eyes meet those of The Sun God, one eye a golden yellow, the other a pale translucent grey a distinctive colouration shared with those he favours, Hathor, Horus, Isis, Osiris, the ones he trusts the most. When Seth looks into his great-great-uncle's eyes it is a reminder of his status, outcast, murderer of his brother, each day he must be reminded of his guilt. He knows he will never be well loved by the leader of the pantheon, he knows he must always be apart and different.

Ra knows it too, and is saddened.

Seth shrugs, 'How much longer must this farce continue, how many more aeons must I wait before you decide I have made amends?'

'For that which you inflicted on your brother? Your sentence is not nearly served, Seth.'

The Sun god moves on, towards a group of elder gods; Sobek, Khnum, Ptah, Neith, only Naith shows vigour and vitality. She approaches her son, the accoutrements of war set about her person; shield, bows and arrows. 'How fares it?' She says.

'As always mother, as you are strong in the world, so am I.'

'As long as all these nephews and nieces of yours continue to bicker amongst themselves shall I prosper.'

'Their bickering now goes beyond simple rivalry, they crave worship, and they wish for sacrifices, worship requires sacrifice. The humans must prove themselves worthy of the divine blessings they have been given. The surrender of their mortal lives is that proof, as they perish, so we thrive and constant conflict on their world supplies a convenient means of their dying.' Ra hesitates as he intones the age old mantra, he says the words, but he isn't sure he believes them. Not anymore.

'Am I complaining?' Neith's laughter rattles her weapons. 'Of course not, I am full of power, unlike those wraiths I needs must spend most of my time with.'

The three elder gods, to a lesser extent Ptah, are truly shadows of their former selves, sallow and emaciated. It is hard to imagine that once they received the adoration of humans, soaking in the worship, imbibing the blood of sacrificed beasts, glowing with the flames of the ritual pyres lit in their names. For now they linger feebly, clinging to the pale existence, little to say and less to do.

Looking at the three, Ra knows that even gods may fade; even gods may one day die.

HORUS

Late in the day the squabbling siblings and their children came, Osiris, his body rebuilt, covered in bandages, blood seeping through, staining the wrappings. Clinging to him his sister-wife Isis, holding her hand, Nephthys.

The Lady of the house reluctantly leaves her sister to join her brother-husband. Seth greets her coldly, Nephthys simpers in his heartless embrace, but in her eyes is the yearning to be elsewhere.

Her son, her solitary offspring, Anubis, arrives to give worship to Ra, scowling and brooding; he stands apart, aloof, arms crossed. Seth nods once to him, the Jackal headed one nods back, an imperceptible movement of his head.

Following closely behind comes his cousin and half brother Horus, with his four children scampering and brawling around his feet, paying little heed to the other gods with whom they frequently and violently collide. Horus has but one eye, the other covered by an elaborate patch; he winks his good eye at Ra in greeting.

Seth snaps at Horus, 'Keep those noisy brats of yours under control,' his hissing, echoing voice a snarling curse.

Horus glares back at him, enough venom in his single eye to fill two, 'Have you a yearning for me to rip from your crotch those little gonads of yours once again, you red headed freak?' He hooks his hand, gripping an imaginary pair of balls.

'Try it and lose the other eye, moron.'

None of them stay long, their visit more out of duty than love, some exchange pleasantries, masking the divisions between them.

They seem ill at ease thinks Ra, perhaps they sense what I sense, that our days are numbered and it troubles them, or worse, that it troubles them not.

The solar barque has almost reached the western gate of heaven, Ra must soon leave Meseket, and with only the stoic, silent Aker for company, return on the black barque Mandet through the utter darkness of the netherworld. No sleep, no rest, utter spectral seclusion to balance the brilliance of the day.

THOTH

Thoth, his adviser, his dear friend he is always glad to see. The two of them repair to the stern of the barque, there only Ma'at can overhear their quiet conversation.

'Tell me something old friend, something to lift this dark cloud from my brow,' Ra says.

'You are not dead, Ra, no matter how dull and dim becomes your life. Remember oblivion is worse, that you must never forget.'

'Ha, I feel a chill though, why?'

'We near the river's end, the day has passed, the night approaches.'

'No, no it is none of that, I fear for the future, a fear inside, a cold prickling in my heart. I fear, Thoth. I don't know why.'

Thoth looked deep into the Sun god's eyes, 'We are old, you and I, Ra. Time grows short for us. The future is a strange beast, the less of it that is left, the more we fear it.'

'Is that then what it is I feel?

'Only you can answer that, my old friend, only you can know for certain.'

THE DEATH BLOW

The meeting place of the Gods

'How long?' he asked, sitting up in the comfort pod and rotating his body towards the diminutive figure crouching at the foot of the steps.

'Four Units,' she replied, her voice a deep pleasurable purr. 'All recording equipment has been laid and has been functioning correctly for the past twenty units Lord.'

'That is excellent, come, let us assemble the others.' He stood, and then turned towards the arch dividing the vast hemispheres of the dome. His form clad entirely in white, the flowing robes setting off the multi-coloured domed crown that appeared as an integral part of his visage. His sharply hooked golden beak and staring pale eyes matching the stylised golden cobra that adorned his forehead.

'Is this the end then?' His excitement obvious in the tremor that resonated through his deep bass voice.

'So we believe my Lord Ra,' a whispered reply from Ma'at.

Ra, god of the sun drifted through the opening, walking on air a foot from the shimmering floor. As he entered, from the black crystal flooring rose twenty four thrones. He made his way to the most elegant, constructed entirely of emerald green jasper, and arranging his robes, sat. A rainbow materialised behind the throne.

The first of his closest companions, Bastet the goddess with the face of a cat arranged herself, curling around the sun god's feet. Ma'at the healer, with the feather in her hair moved to his right. His third companion detached herself from her partner Bes, and walked silently across the shimmering flooring, Hathor with the gentle face of a calf, stood by the throne to his left. The last of the companions to join him, Ra's alter ego, almost his twin, Horus, the falcon headed god of war, son of Isis, stood behind the Sun god.

The four opened the heavens with a chant, their voices in unison echoing around the chamber, 'Sunda, Sanda, Sonda, Khema ko Loder, -- what was, what is, and what is to be, is yet to come.' The four companions rose and gave worship on their knees to the sun god saying, 'You alone are worthy Ra to receive honour, glory and power. Reincarnation of Amun, you are father of all.'

From around the thrones came a mighty fanfare of thundering and brilliant flashes of lightning to summoning the lesser gods. Ra's four companions prostrated themselves before him once more.'

They rose and resumed their places. Others began to make their entrances. From across time and space they came, arriving in their comfort pods, arranging themselves in order of superiority around the creators.

Sekhmet the goddess of war and destruction, alongside her Thoth, the god of wisdom with the long beak and head of an Ibis, between them walked a beautiful, diminutive human female. No common slave this, for she carried herself with the deportment of one of authority. The sight of her caused consternation amongst the lesser gods, but none dared challenge Sekhmet, for 'the wrath of Ra' walked with her sickle exposed.

Others walked amongst them, Nut, queen of the skies dressed in blue, Anubis, god of the dead; his jackal head towering above the other gods. Beside him walked the dwarf god Bes, his lion mane resplendent, standing around his head like a halo. Hathor, daughter of Ra, the goddess of love, smiled as she watched them approach.

Bes stepped to Q'rem who matched him in height, the strange features of the dwarf god smiled at her. Bes raised his right hand and touched Q'rem between her eyes with a stubby fore finger. 'WE

MEET AT LAST CHOSEN ONE.' He sent, and then turned to take the throne beside his wife Hathor.

~

Last of all came four of the children of the Ennead of Heliopolis; the OGDOAD, Isis mincing sinuously, her swinging hips accentuating her slim body, arm clinging to her brother/husband Osiris the ruler of the underworld, his grotesque form as always, wrapped in funereal bandages. Their siblings followed, walking apart; Nephthys, her winged arms crossed in front of her body, her brother/husband Seth the chaos lord, resplendent in black strode arrogantly. The four took their thrones in silence, ignored by the greater gods who had arranged themselves in the seats closest to Ra.

'So it begins,' said Ra softly, his eyes on the wide angle vista that had replaced his view of the facing wall. The watchers followed his gaze.

~

Millions upon millions of tons of rock travelling at thousands of miles per second struck the far side of the moon, but this time it was no glancing blow. The moon shuddered and shook. A great cloud of debris rose almost ethereally around her. Blood red, the dust flowed like a windswept veil, held only by the weak Luna gravity and refracting the reflected sunlight. The ichors of the mortally wounded moon flowed outward, surrounding her in a sickly halo.

The Queen of the night began to move, pushed from her orbit she crept imperceptibly towards her larger partner. As she moved she began to rotate. Vistas gazed upon only by astronauts, and those who had poured over the many photographs they brought back with them, became visible. Her face; known, loved, and on the lips of minstrels for thousands of years, was changing, the familiar markings disappeared, hidden forever, in their place a huge piece of another moon could be seen, embedded into her.

Closer and closer Luna came, until she filled a quarter of the sky, but by then no-one remained to gaze in wonder upon her new face.

Floods and earthquakes, tsunamis thousands of feet high swept away all that puny man had built and laboured over. Volcanoes belched thick sulphurous smoke that darkened the sky. Meteors, pieces of the moon captured by the earth's gravity, screamed like burning hail through the thick black clouds.

~

Seth stood and strode from the auditorium, '!T IS DONE!' He cried out in victory, as he disappeared.

RETURN OF LIFE

It was a thousand frozen years while Ra mourned the planet and hid his face from its surface. A thousand years before once more he shone his gaze on the tortured stricken world, a thousand more before the air could be deemed safe to breathe, and yet a millennium more for the Earth to be born again. In a moment of compassion for the dead planet that she always loved, Nut, mother of the gods, brought seeds for both plants and creatures; she disseminated them from above as she bridged the sky. Life breathed and green sprouted once more across the earth and in the seas.

Life spawned and grew; not in the multiplicity that had once flourished, but sufficient to maintain a balance. Crawlers, Wrigglers, Buzzers and Stingers, insects and arachnids ruled where man, reptiles and mammals had once strutted supreme. Without restrictions they multiplied, preying upon each other, growing far beyond their once puny sizes.

Changing, adapting to their new environment, they flourished.

Q'REM'S REVELATIONS

'Sekhi, did that lot really happen?' Q'rem asked the giant goddess, her mind re-living the horror of the earth's demise.

'YES, MY DEAR ONE, IT DID.'

'When?'

'WHEN IS NOT THE CORRECT CONCEPT, FOR TIME HAS NO RELEVANCE, WE ARE OUTSIDE OF TIME, AS ARE YOU AT THIS MOMENT.'

'How come? I must have been with you for at least six months.'

'RELATIVE TO THE TIME FRAME YOU OCCUPIED BEFORE PASSING ACROSS THE VOID, YES. BUT YOU COULD RETURN TO THE SECOND YOU DEPARTED, OR EVEN DAYS, WEEKS, MONTHS AND EVEN YEARS BEFORE THAT MOMENT, AND CONVERSELY TO ANY TIME FOLLOWING THAT MOMENT. BUT I AGREE WITH YOU, YOU WILL BE SIX MONTHS OLDER IF YOU WERE TO LEAVE THE VOID, BECAUSE AGE IS RELATIVE AND CONTINUOUS.'

'Yeah, but when does that catastrophe take place?'

'THAT I CANNOT ANSWER. ONLY THE DESTROYER KNOWS THE MOMENT WHEN HE WILL RETURN ONCE MORE TO CRUSH RA'S CATTLE IN ORDER THAT HE MIGHT CONTINUE HIS BATTLE WITH HORUS.'

'So there's a chance it hasn't happened yet?' Q'rem's voice rose at least an octave. 'And I wish you wouldn't call us that.'

Sekhmet laughed, a throaty chuckle, 'BUT YOU ARE, FOR HUMANS AS YOU CALL YOURSELVES, WERE SEEDED BY RA HIMSELF.'

'I haven't got my head round that bit yet. Something has been bugging me, if you guys are so omnipotent, living forever, etcetera,

etcetera, how come you guys got such backward ideas on day and night and all that type of stuff?

'BECAUSE MY PRECIOUS LITTLE FRIEND WE ARE OUTSIDE OF TIME, A DAY OR A THOUSAND YEARS MEANS NOTHING TO US, WE CONVERSE IN THE WAY WE ALWAYS HAVE, WE ENJOY THE WHOLE CONCEPT OF THE SIMPLE, EVEN THOUGH WE UNDERSTAND THE MINUTIAE OF THE COSMOS.'

'Those little boats of yours, do you need them to travel through the stars?'

'THEY ARE BUT COMFORT PODS MY DEAR. OUR MOVEMENT THROUGH SPACE AND TIME IS INSTANTANEOUS FOR OUR ABILITY TO TRAVEL COMES FROM OUR MINDS.

'So do have I a future then?'

'YOU HAVE A FUTURE; LET US LEAVE IT THERE FOR I CANNOT SEE EVERYTHING.'

'Strange honey pie, I find that a little bit difficult to believe.'

'NOT ALL OF US KNOW ABOUT THAT WHICH IS TO COME. I, LIKE YOU CAN LIVE ONLY IN ONE PLANE AT ONE TIME.'

'What about yon Armageddon movie we watched then?'

'AS I SAID Q'REM, 'NOT ALL OF US', MEANS THAT SOME CAN. YOU HAVE LEARNT MUCH, I THINK IT MAY BE TIME FOR YOUR RETURN'

'But what will I do? I'll miss you so much.'

'RA HAS DECREED THAT I SHOULD ACCOMPANY YOU AT ALL TIMES, I WILL GO WITH YOU, AS YOUR GUIDE, PROTECTOR AND FRIEND.'

Q'rem beamed; she rushed to the seated goddess, and planted a kiss upon her furry cheek.

A CELEBRATION IS PLANNED

What's the celebration for? Lord Bes said it was going to be a right ding dong, piss up.'

The giant chuckled, 'You have an amusing turn of phrase sweet one.' Her face turned serious for a moment and she looked down at the girl, ''Tis not a pretty tale, are you sure you wish to hear it?'

'Bring it on babe, if it gets too much I can always cry off.'

'So be it Q'rem, before I begin; I ask for your forgiveness.' she sat on a low stool beside the standing human, her eyes level with Q'rem's, a tear rolled down her muzzle.

'What ever it is you have to tell me, I'm sure you had good reason at the time.' Q'rem threw her arms about the massive head and kissed the tear away. 'I love you Sekhi.'

~

The lioness began to sing, her voice a beautiful rich contralto;

'Mine is a heart of carnelian, crimson as murder on a holy day.
Mine is a heart of corneal, the gnarled roots of a dogwood and the bursting of flowers.
I am the broken wax seal on my lover's letters.
I am the phoenix, the fiery sun, consuming and resuming myself.
I will what I will.
Mine is a heart of carnelian, blood red as the crest of a phoenix.'

'There was a time when humans entered into a conspiracy to overthrow the Gods. They blasphemed against Ra, king of gods and men, heretical priests and magicians plotted ways to turn against the Gods for their destruction, using those powers the gods had given to men that they might flourish and grow great upon the earth. Ra, hearing of this plan, called to meet with him the most ancient and potent Deities, those who had been with him in the primeval waters before the time when with his eye, the sun, he had made life. The gods counselled together and it was decided that I, being the force against which no other force can prevail, would appear on the earth and quell the rebellion. I would manifest and punish all those who had held in their minds evil images and imagined wicked plots.

'Then I walked among men and destroyed them and drank their blood. Night after night I waded in blood, slaughtering humans, tearing and rending their bodies and drinking their blood. The other gods decided that the slaughter was enough and should stop, but they could find no way to stop me, for I was drunk on human blood. The carnage went on, the gods recognized that my rage sustained by intoxication, would mercilessly cause me to proceed with the killing until the last human life had been extinguished.

'Then Ra had brought to him from the world known as Elephantine certain plants, which included Solanaceae which is brewed as a powerful mind-altering drug. Those plants, and possibly opium or hemp, were sent to the god Sekti at Heliopolis. Sekti added these drugs to a mixture of beer and human blood until seven thousand jugs of the substance had been made. The jars were taken to a place where I would pass and were poured out onto the ground, inundating the fields for a great distance. And when I came to these fields I perceived what I thought to be more blood. I rejoiced and drank all of the liquid, at the last drop I collapsed insensible, and slept for a hundred years. When I awoke my heart was filled with joy, my mind was changed and I thought no more of destroying mankind.

'After that, Ra named me as the 'One Who Comes in Peace,' praising my beauty and charm. I am depicted on your world as a woman with the head of a lioness - I wonder why?' she chuckled a growling purr that Q'rem had grown to love so much and continued in a lighter tone; 'Occasionally they adorn me with a sun disk attesting to my father's greatness. I boast not when I say that there are more large statues and paintings of me than of any other deity. I am known as the Great One of Healing. I am a paradox on Earth for I am seen as the Goddess of War and the Goddess of Love. I am seen as an underworld deity because of my destructive tendencies. They believe that I have the power to completely destroy not only human bodies, but their souls - total destruction. Additionally, they call me the protector of the dead in the underworld. I am frequently named the Avenger of Wrongs and the Scarlet Lady, a reference to all that blood, and thus I am seen as ruling over menstruation.

The Celebration has many times included wild orgies which have earned me the additional titles of Great Harlot and Lady of the Scarlet-Coloured Garments. The celebration includes drinking of the exact substance given to me to quench my blood thirst - obviously without the blood. Its potency though is not reduced.'

'Now I understand,' Q'rem gave her another fierce hug, 'I know why that fekin huge sickle of yours scares me shitless.'

ROB'S DREAM

We three lovers were given a home-dome of our own for our stay in Brimat. We re-kindled our love in a most enjoyable way. George without the girls for over a year was most pleased to get re-acquainted with them and together we proved that our love for one another had not diminished in any way. Whilst we lay luxuriating in the afterglow of our lovemaking, entwined in a knot of arms and legs, I broached the subject of our children. Immediately I was inundated with images of both babies. Unable to contain my new abilities any longer, I wrapped them in my arms and without a moment's pause, jumped to our bed in the M'ntar caves.

We three, naked as jaybirds swiftly dressed ourselves in clothing the girls had placed on shelves they had built around the cave. They surely had not been idle in my absence, as there were many different changes of clothing for all three of us, beautifully crafted from fine hides.

Now that we were for the first time naked, and in full daylight, the two remarked on the purple hue of my skin, the purple colour of my eyes and hair. I had no answer for them, other than it could only be related to my having bonded with the Purple Queen.

Dressed, we walked arm in arm with me in the middle, through the cave to introduce me to our babies.

~

After the joy of seeing the two boys, and spending some hours with them whilst their mothers bathed, fed and settled them down, I was exhausted. The girls chose to spend more time with the children, but I made my way back to the comfort of the depression in the cave floor. Nice as it was, the bed in the home-dome was too soft for my liking. The soft shed skin had been replaced.

I immediately fell into a deep sleep; my dreams were of an earlier time, another ancestor from a bygone age...

GUSTENAI

A party of riders numbering a score reached the boundary of the town of Gustenai.
~
At the south of the forest of Denna to the west of the hills which bore the same name, Gustenai sat quietly; her population like the forest, strong and silent, living a gentle artisan life; carpenters, builders, woodsmen and hunters, easy living folk, using their hands to wrest a livelihood from the land and the forest, employing skills passed down from father to son, mother to daughter.

The folks of Gustenai were quiet spoken; they stepped with a silent tread and interfered not in another's business.

It had been more than a year since so many visitors had come from the outside world; those within the town came out from their homes and businesses to watch the riders as they approached.

They rode slowly and confidently, as if they owned all they surveyed. There was no mistaking them for who they were; the black robes and breastplates a palpable sign, even without the blazing skull set in the centre of the latter, to definitively mark them as Witch Finders from the Church at Naridge.

They wore round black leather helmets atop their shaven heads, save for the lead rider, whose thick blonde hair was draped with a black hood.

The riders were clean-shaven, as were all those who served directly under the Bishop. This was not a personal choice, but a purposeful decision. For Bishop Boel sported no beard.

DEATH RIDES IN

Not three months previously another priest of the same order had ridden alone into the town. He had demanded The Nag's Head be demolished as a place of sin and debauchery, and the space that remained utilised for a church to be built, and that all the heathen, barbarian residents of Gustenai, should bow down before him, the representative of Bishop Boel, and confess their sins. At the same time donating to the Bishop's coffers, by way of a full tithe, lest they be damned to the everlasting hell-fires for all eternity.

Without hesitation the young men of Gustenai dunked him first in a barrel of warm (it might have been hot) pitch, then rolled him in stinking dung and chicken feathers and dispatched him, sitting backwards on an old mule back in the general direction of Naridge.

~

The Master WitchFinder reined his magnificent pure black mount to a halt in front of the little gathering and dismounted, passing his reins to the closest guardcleric. He announced in a stentorian voice; 'I have irrefutable proof that amongst you are men who committed a grievous crime. Firstly as ring-leader, I call forth Robert, son of Dorian, present immediately yourself to me. Know that I am Brother Sinseeker, Master WitchFinder of this region for the great and holy Bishop Boel of Naridge. I have come to ascertain the depths of your guilt and thereby judge that which is required to redeem your soul.' He paused, then added, 'and, after that, the souls of the other miscreants who assisted you in desecrating the mission of our emissary, will be examined.'

ROBERT ACCUSED

Yvetta Jom, the merchant's daughter, was torn between running to Robert and warning him of the WitchFinder's arrival, but she did not want to miss whatever Brother Sinseeker might further say. Archer, Robert's true and best friend stood beside her. The young man's face dropped at the announcement, for he too had been responsible for the treatment metered out to the pompous priest.

Several townsters, perhaps alerted by the Master WitchFinder's loud voice, had stepped out of their homes to find out what was ado. Brother Sinseeker acknowledged them with an occasional wave and a pious nod as he strode commandingly toward the town square.

The sky rumbled, but otherwise the late summer's day seemed oddly calm. There was not even the least puff of wind blowing from the snow capped mountains, in itself something unusual for the time of year.

As Yvetta entered the town square following the others, she felt as if the spirits of the dead stood hushed around her in the shapes of the other townsfolk.

After visiting the town Captain's jail, occasionally home to a riotous drunk or two. The WitchFinder marched across the square and stopped before the town's premier hostelry and repeated his demand.

Inside, even the sounds of celebration were not sufficient to drown out his voice.

A pair of the town's constables crashed through the door, and rounded on Robert, as he began making his way to answer the summons. 'Robert! Come with us,' barked the taller of the two, a plain-faced young man whom Robert knew as Captain Lockout's nephew, Downsword. 'Don't give us no problems, huh?'

In response, the woodsman as indicated quietly placed his hands behind his back and turned so the town guards may secure his wrists. When they had so done, they led him out. Lockout met them at the door. The captain made no attempt to hide his unease, although he did not bother to explain to Robert the reason for his mood. The woodsman could only assume that for some reason it boded ill for him.

As soon as he stepped out Robert knew that matters had gone from bad to worse than worse. He observed the senior figure from the Church of Light, and immediately knew him to be more than simply an itinerant priest from the nearest town.

This was a Master WitchFinder, one of the highest-ranking officials of the sect. Worse, the imperious-looking man was accompanied by a troop of brooding guardclerics. Amongst the small crowd, he noticed a distraught Yvetta accompanied by Archer, he had last seen them both at the beginning of his wedding celebration.

The priest strode up to him. Gazing down his nose at the woodsman, he declared in a much-too-loud voice, 'Robert, son of Dorian, know that I am Brother Sinseeker, Master WitchFinder of this land for the great and golden Bishop Boel. I come to ascertain the depths of your guilt and thereby judge that which is required to redeem your heathen soul.'

Robert went white. Brother Sinseeker had left little or no doubt that he considered the matter of a trial moot. Before he could even open his mouth to protest, the Master WitchFinder turned from him to where the captain himself looked on with slightly more enthusiasm than Robert would have liked.

'With your permission, Captain Lockout, we shall make use of your quarters for the questioning of this one. Through the Bishop, blessed be he, I carry the necessary authority for this situation; even the Governor Fiscal himself would accept my good word.'

From the Master WitchFinder's tone, thought Robert, Lockout and the rest should rely on it too, whether he liked the fact or not. Considering how Brother Sinseeker had so far handled the matter, Robert doubted he would be allowed to say much in his defence, unless he chose to confess, 'but what is my crime?' Robert bit back the question. Brother Sinseeker would not be denied. Robert tried to console himself with the fact that at least Constance, his bride of less than an hour, had not been included.

That, the woodsman could not have borne.

BROTHER SINSEEKER

An incomer to Gustenai merely a month past, they had fallen deeply in love the moment she first arrived. She had already suffered much at the sect's hands, escaping from Gni-nnut, accused of witchcraft or was it beauty, her parents tortured to confess of her sins.

Even as he thought of that, out of the corner of his eye, the telltale emerald green of her bridal garments flashed. The woodsman shook with dismay.

Without meaning to, Robert had glanced in his new wife's direction. Unfortunately, so did the Master WitchFinder. Constance stood like an animal caught in a trap. She appeared to have crept from around the back of the Nag's Head to watch things unfold, and no doubt her fear for Robert had made her forget his warning to hide.

Brother Sinseeker could obviously see from her blonde locks that she was not a local, for the people of Gustenai were dark of hair and countenance. That in itself might not have mattered, but there was that in his gaze, which when it met hers, that seemed to register some recognition. The robed figure thrust a condemning finger at the woman. 'You there, you...'

~

The sky thundered, this time with such vehemence that several people, including Brother Sinseeker, had to cover their ears.

A powerful wind rose up howling like a hungry wolf. People were thrust back by the intensity, even several of the WitchFinder's clericguards unable to hold their positions, staggered and grasped at their compatriots for support. Only two figures remained somewhat unmoved, at least momentarily, by the fearsome blast of wind. Robert and Constance.

~

But the Master WitchFinder had to struggle to maintain his dignity. He tore his eyes from Constance, returning them to the prisoner. Robert's expression was terrible to behold. Brother Sinseeker's eyed the woodsman with what seemed both fury and fear. 'By the Bishop's smock! You are a witch.'

A savage bolt of lightning struck the town centre and Master WitchFinder. He had no time to scream. A sickening, burning stench filled the air, dispersed quickly by the wind. The bolt left a charred mass.

Robert had seen the results of other strikes, but none with the intensity of this. A second bolt struck near the first, people began scattering in every direction. The wind continued to howl through Gustenai, bowling over those not holding on to something solid. Robert looked for Constance, but she was nowhere to be found. A piece of rubbish flew up at his face and the woodsman instinctively blocked it with his arm.

Only then did he notice that he was free. The ropes dangled loosely on one wrist, he tugged at them and they blew away with the billowing dust.

ARCHER AND YVETTA

Archer saw the trader running toward them, however, standing behind the hunter, Yvetta did not notice Jom, nor could she hear her father calling to her.

At that moment, a massive fragment of roof tore from the town constables' headquarters; it fluttered in the air like a gigantic bird, and then dropped with all the accuracy of an executioner's axe, following the unsuspecting Jom as he fought to cross the street.

Archer shouted, but could not be heard over the gale. A chill coursed through him. The hunter knew that there was only one choice left. He leapt for Yvetta, tackling her about the waist, much in the way he would a critter seeking to escape from one of his traps. The archer did not care that he had shattered all rules of impropriety; all that mattered was keeping the trader's daughter from witnessing the horrifying scene. There was nothing he could do for Jom for he was too far away.

But although he managed to mask her view, Archer could do nothing for his own. He watched in macabre fascination as the piece of roof caught Jom from behind. The force with which it struck the back of the man's neck ensured that there would be no hope for him. The sharp edge severed bone and flesh with horrifying ease, and despite the fact that he could hear nothing but the wind, the veteran hunter knew exactly what Jom's terrible beheading would have sounded like.

The remainder of the broken piece continued its crazy path across the square. Yvetta chose that moment to finally struggle free. She looked up at Archer, her expression one of surprise, and perhaps a little embarrassment, if her reddening cheeks were any sign. Archer suddenly felt uncomfortable, and not merely from having witnessed the horrific fate of her father.

'Let me up, please,' she said her voice barely audible. 'Have you seen Robert?'

CONSTANCE

Not wasting time considering the carelessness of his guards, and still confused, Robert attempted to focus on his next move. However, Brother Sinseeker's escort decided matters for him by battling to reach the woodsman despite the gale force wind. Three of them were already almost within weapon's range. But, as the first reached him, a thick wooden bench that Robert knew usually sat in front of the tavern, flew past him. With perfect aim, the bench collided with two of the guards, sending one flying, the other was squished, a bloody mess crushed against the jail wall. The third decided discretion was the finer part of valour, and ran back to the jail searching for cover.

Some distance behind the sprawling figures, Constance reappeared. Holding on to the corner of the smithy with one hand, she waved for Robert to come to her with the other.

Without hesitation, the stunned woodsman ran toward his new bride. All around him, loose objects whistled through the air. People scurried into buildings. Another lightning bolt struck near the town jail, tearing apart most of its exterior stone walls.

Despite the many flying terrors, Robert made it to Constance unscathed. Other than a few loose strands of golden hair, the woman, too, appeared untouched. Concern for her overwhelmed all other thoughts. 'Constance, you must find shelter!' He exclaimed.

She seized his arm, but instead of coming with him to the stables' entrance, she tugged

Robert toward the woods. Her strength surprised him, but rather than risk a struggle that would leave both of them in the open, the woodsman allowed her to guide them both beyond Gustenai.

He knew that common sense better dictated that they hide in some building, but Robert allowed himself to be convinced that they would surely find as safe a hidey-hole in the forest.

ARCHER AND YVETTA

The hunter's own mortification grew. Unaware of Jom's tragic end, Yvetta's first thoughts had gone to the woodsman and no one else. Certainly not Archer.

Still, her concern for the woodsman gave him a momentary reprieve from relating what had occurred. Now was not the time for Yvetta to know. Besides, if she saw her father's body in the midst of this insane weather, it was possible that she would rush to his body, and end up joining him in an early grave.

'I saw him run toward the stables,' he shouted in response to her question. Archer had to repeat himself before the trader's daughter understood completely. He pulled her to her feet, careful to avoid turning her in the direction of the grisly sight. 'Hold my hand tight or you will be blown back.'

To his relief, Yvetta obeyed without question. Archer dragged her in the direction he had last seen his friend, the violent wind buffeting at them like a wild animal on heat. He did not know what they would do if and when they actually located Robert. The woodsman was considered a prisoner, a possible desecrator in the eyes of some. Archer's duty should have been to either convince his friend to return and they would face justice together, failing that, force him to do so. But the hunter had already seen enough of what had passed for justice, and the thought of turning Robert over to the WitchFinders' or even to Lockout, left Archer cold.

More importantly, if he brought Robert back to Gustenai to face charges, the archer had no doubt that he would forever blacken himself in the eyes of the woodsman's cousin Yvetta.

They raced for the edge of the town even as others ran past them in diverse directions.

Planks tore from buildings along with slates from roofs, adding to the dangerous debris flying about. With relief, he plunged Jom's daughter and himself into the greensward.

Immediately noticing the difference between the weather there, and the mad turbulence in Gustenai.

It was almost as if he had shut a door behind them. The foliage barely shook and the wind had all but ceased. Despite all, the hunter did not slow until the two of them were well away from the town's border. Only then did Archer pause, near an ancient oak, and that more for his companion's sake than his own.

'Are you okay?' he asked her.

Gasping for breath after the desperate run, Yvetta nodded. Her gaze shifted around, seeking Robert, cousin or no, she had adored the big woodsman since childhood and had always yearned secretly that he would take her to be his wife. Her absence from the wedding celebration a chance to still her weeping at his loss to the blonde incomer.

CHARLES

The wind had abated enough for people to move about once more, without being cast into mortal danger. A sharp point caught him in the small of his back. He started to turn, only to be seized roughly by more than one pair of powerful hands. The stern face of a WitchFinder guardcleric came within inches of his. 'You,' barked the figure. 'You are kin to that accused heretic and wizard, Robert. Admit it. You have been identified as his brother.'

Still struggling to comprehend whatever was happening, Charles mutely nodded. 'Wizard? ... Wizard? What Wizard?' ran through his befuddled mind.

Unfortunately, that proved to be his captor's cue to drag him through the town's square, toward where a group of locals stood pensively eyeing four other WitchFinder guardclerics who stood with swords unsheathed daring them to move. Charles estimated nearly twenty people in the group, their wide eyes and movements reminded him of a flock of sheep being herded towards a slaughter house.

Lockout stood arguing with one of the minions of the Church. Of his nephew, there was no sign. A pair of his constables stood near, but they looked uncertain as what to do, if anything. 'But you've no right to be holding these good people,' the town captain insisted.

'Under the authority granted by the secret agreements between Bishop Boel and the Church of Light we have every right we need or desire,' blustered the guard. To the captain's men, he added, 'and under that law; the authority of your captain is now ours. You will obey all orders of the Church, and the first is to remove your captain to his quarters and confine him there.'

One of the locals put a tentative hand toward Lockout. 'What about us?'

'And if I won't move?' demanded Lockout.

'Then, if you disobey, I will have no choice but to have some of my own men deal with you, and then them afterwards.' He gestured towards the prisoners. The captain glanced at the fearsome warriors, then at his own pathetic Guard. Shaking his head, he reluctantly turned and allowed the latter to lead him away.

A POWER RELEASED

Indeed, the wind seemed to lessen as they rushed deeper into the woods. Refuse still swept past them, but, miraculously, nothing greater than a leaf touched them. From the direction of Gustenai came the now-familiar crashing sound of thunder. Robert started to look over his shoulder, but Constance tugged him ever forward.

Thunder continued to rumble as if a thousand horses galloped across the sky.

The woodsman's thoughts went to the WitchFinders and the unfortunate Brother Sinseeker. The guards would surely be after him once the weather settled, especially after the unsettling death of their commander.

Robert blamed the cleric's horrific end on the mercurial aspects of nature, even though never in his life had the woodsman witnessed such a bizarre and deadly change, he did not doubt that somehow Brother Sinseeker's fate would be tied to him, no matter how crazy that might seem.

'Keep running!' Constance called, looking back over her shoulder at him. 'Keep running!' But in her concern for him, his bride paid no attention to her own steps. Robert saw the dip in the forest floor before her foot slipped into it. He tried to shout a warning, but by then his bride was already falling.

Her grip on his hand slipped. With a little gasp escaping her lips Constance tumbled forward. As she landed, she twisted about, this time with an agonized cry. Stumbling, Robert went to her side. Constance laid there, her eyes open but momentarily unseeing.

'Constance!' All fear of the unnerving weather or the WitchFinder guards vanished. All that mattered to the woodsman was the figure sprawled before him.

To his great relief, the woman blinked. Her eyes focused again. She looked up at Robert and her expression made him redden.

Trying to cover up his embarrassment, Robert gave her a hand. However, as Constance tried to stand, she let out a moan and her right ankle buckled. 'I think ... I think it may be twisted,' she managed. 'Can you see?'

Robert lifted her skirts, he could feel his face blush, wife or not, this was all new to him. Her ankle was red and swollen, sprained, possibly broken. He touched the puffy red skin expecting her to cry out, but she lay silent. Then for some reason unknown to him, he grasped her ankle gently and held it with both hands, feeling it throb. A low moan escaped her lips, he looked at her face, it was not pain that he saw written there, but something else. Shocked, he looked again at her ankle, finding instead that it now appeared perfectly healthy.

'But...' Robert stared at the limb, certain that his eyes deceived him. At the least, the ankle had been badly bruised, and now it was not.

He looked to Constance, and the way in which she gazed at him only made Robert more uncomfortable. There was awe, incredible awe, and what almost seemed like worship? 'You turned your eyes away,' the woman murmured. 'But you left your hands on my ankle. I knew, I felt you touching me, but I suddenly... I felt a wonderful warmth and the pain? It went away.'

'That's not possible; there must be a reasonable explanation. An injury like that doesn't heal itself, nor in a moment.'

'You did it.'

At first he thought that he had not heard Constance correctly. Then, when her words at last registered with him, Robert could scarcely believe that the young woman would even consider something so outrageous. 'I'm no mage or witch,' he insisted, taken aback. 'Your ankle was obviously not hurt after all. That's the only answer.'

She shook her head; eyes filled with something that should have gladdened his soul but only unnerved him more. Adoration. 'No! I know the pain I felt. I know what I sensed from your hand, and I know that all the pain disappeared as if it had never been.'

Robert stepped back from her. 'But I didn't do it.'

The blond woman rose, then stepped toward him. Constance moved without the least sign of injury. 'Then who? Who performed the miracle?'

The last word sent shivers through him. He would not listen to her. 'We've no time for such foolishness.' He looked up. The sky seemed calmer, at least near to them. Thunder yet roiled in the direction of Gustenai. Another bolt flashed over the town. 'The storm,' Robert had no other word for the peculiar weather, 'seems to be stalled. Praise be for that bit of luck.'

'I do not think it was luck,' the woman murmured.

'Then what...?' The woodsman cut off, his face blanching. 'No, Constance, don't even jest.'

'But do you not see, Robert? How timely was that wind. How righteous was that bolt that struck Brother Sinseeker before he could condemn you for crimes you did not commit.'

'And now you'd claim I've powers that have slain a man? Think of that, woman.' For the first time since he had met her, Robert was afraid to be near Constance. It was not that he did not find her desirable, but surely she suffered from dementia. Perhaps the strain caused by her recent misfortunes had finally taken its toll. That had to be the explanation for her behaviour. But what explained the injury that Robert had seen? He did not consider himself of an imaginative nature. How, then, could his mind have conjured up such an elaborate delusion?

'No.' the woodsman snapped at himself. If he followed such reasoning, he would find himself believing Constance's outlandish suggestion. If that happened, it would be better for him to turn himself in to the WitchFinders or the Town Guard before he truly did endanger someone else.

A soft, warm touch on his hand stirred him back to the moment. Constance stood barely an inch from him. 'I know it was you who healed me, Robert, and I believe that it is you who summoned the wind and the lightning in our time of need.'

'Constance, please. Listen to the absurdity of what you say.'

Her flawless face filled his vision. 'You want me to believe otherwise? Then prove me wrong.' His young bride gently took him by the chin and turned his head so that his gaze fell upon Gustenai. 'The lightning still falls. The sky still roars its anger at the false accusations made against you. The wind howls at the presumption of those who would judge you when they themselves are guilty.'

'Stop it, Constance.'

But she would not. In a firm, even defiant voice, Constance said, 'Prove me wrong, dear husband. Will with all your might for the sky to silence, why, even clear the clouds away, and if the thunder and lightning cease not, nor the clouds clear, then I will gladly admit that I was sorely deceived.' Her lower lip stiffened. 'Gladly!'

Robert could not believe that Constance was so deluded that she could even imagine that something even remotely like she suggested was possible. Still, if his bride meant what she said, it was the quickest and easiest way to snap her back to reality. Without another word, the woodsman turned toward the turbulent heavens. Although he could have simply looked at them and pretended to be concentrating, Robert somehow felt that so doing would be a betrayal to his partner even though he was convinced nothing would happen.

And so, the son of Dorian squeezed his eyes shut and thought hard. He wished the violent weather to vanish and the clouds to clear. He tried to take the situation as seriously as he could, even if only for Constance's sake. But he was not surprised when everything remained as it was.

Certain that he had given Constance's delusion as much chance as anyone could have, the woodsman wearily turned back to her. He expected his bride to be distraught, but Constance instead looked only patient.

'I did what you asked and you saw what happened, or didn't,' he said soothingly. 'Now let me take you away from here, Constance. We've got to find a place where you, where we can rest and compose our minds.'

Unfortunately, instead of agreeing, Constance continued to stare past him expectantly. Robert's own patience finally came to an end. Constance had swept his heart away the moment that he had first seen her, but he could not tolerate her delusions any longer. It was for her own good, nothing else. 'Constance, you've to pull yourself together. I did what you asked and...'

'And it came to pass,' she interjected, her face glowing with renewed adoration. Constance gently took hold of the woodsman by his arms and turned him back toward the town. Robert, about to reprimand her further, stopped. His mouth hung open. The sun shone over Gustenai.

ACCUSED

'Move into the circle,' growled one of those who had captured him. Charles stumbled toward the others. Those nearest, the other wedding guests immediately shunned him, pressing against their fellows in their fear. Even those who had known him since childhood looked at Charles as if he were some sort of pariah. Or rather, the brother of one.

'That's him,' said the same constable who had shoved the younger son of Dorian forward. Charles turned to face a guard who, although he was a couple of inches shorter than the young woodsman, and stared down the latter with ease. The broad, rough-hewn face looked more appropriate on a brigand than a representative of a holy order.

'Are you not the brother of the heretic and sorcerer?' demanded the lead cleric in a tone that indicated no response from Charles was necessary. 'Where is this Robert? Answer now and you may be spared his fate.'

'Robert has done nothing.'

'His guilt is proven, his mastery of foul arts unquestionable. His soul is lost, but yours may yet receive absolution. You have but to give him up to us.'

The words sounded absurd to Charles, but the cleric clearly believed everything that he said. Despite the fact that he would be condemning himself, Charles did not hesitate to shake his head. 'We will begin with you, then, and the rest here, all known to have fraternized with the heretic; will learn from your example.'

as quickly as they had tossed him in amongst the others, the clerics then pulled him out. They dragged him to an open space. As the younger woodsman was forced onto his knees, he saw the chief cleric stride across to his horse, there to remove a long whip, rolled up and attached to the saddle.

    The WitchFinder undid the loop binding the whip, enabling the full length of the sinister weapon to flow free. He tested the whip once, the crack it made, shaking Charles worse than the harshest thunder had. Face resolute, the cleric headed back to Charles, who squeezed his eyes tight and prepared for the agony.

ROBERT GIVES IT BACK

'It was a coincidence. That was all. A mere coincidence,' he thought. But as Robert stared toward Gustenai, a niggling doubt ate away at him from within. He recalled again how terrible the injury to Constance's ankle had looked, and then how unmarked it had appeared but moments later. There was the horrific storm that had assailed the town as Brother Sinseeker had begun to condemn him and to threaten Constance. What were the odds of lightning striking so precisely?

'A coincidence,' Robert told himself. 'No more than that.' Yet, even he was not entirely convinced. The woodsman continued to stand there, unable to decide what to do, when a face came unbidden into his thoughts, a face he knew as well as his own. Charles's, and with it came a sense of urgency, of impending threat. With a wordless cry, Robert started back towards Gustenai.

'Robert!' called Constance. 'What is it?'

'My brother,' was all he could say. The need to reach the town before something terrible happened to Charles took over. Robert did not question how he knew that his brother was in danger. All that mattered was preventing Charles from coming to harm, even if it meant being recaptured. Without warning figures appeared before him. Robert prepared himself for a struggle then recognized Archer and Yvetta.

'Robert,' blurted the trader's daughter. 'Praise be that you are not harmed.' She moved to enfold him in her arms.

The archer too began to speak, but despite being glad to see them, Robert did not slow. He sensed time was running out. Without apology, the woodsman pushed past the pair, each frantic beat of his heart a cry to move faster. The edge of the town came into sight. His hopes rose, but from further in echoed a sharp cracking sound that sent a shock of pain across Robert's back.

Gritting his teeth, his breath labouring, the son of Dorian staggered into Gustenai square. The sight that met his gaze filled him with loathing and anger. He saw many of his fellow townsfolk, his close friends, herded together like cattle, their expressions mirroring fear and confusion. Grim WitchFinder guards pointed sharp weapons at them.

But worse, so much worse was that which the townsfolk watched. Near the ruined jail, a WitchFinder guardcleric had Charles on his knees. Another armoured figure made certain that Robert's brother could not rise. Someone had torn open the back of Charles's tunic and a long, red slash adorned his brother's back. A blood filled stripe caused by the guardcleric's scaled whip.

The leading guardcleric noticed Robert, and readied his whip for another strike. 'Surrender yourself, wizard, or you will force me to cause your brother even more pain.' His twisted words, insisting that it would be Robert's fault if Charles was again lashed only made the older woodsman more furious. He wanted to smash out at them in the way that they had whipped his brother.

The length of the WitchFinder's whip, as if blown by a gust of wind flew straight into the air. Startled, he pulled at it, trying to bring it down, but the cord instead flew and wrapped around his neck. He clawed and scrabbled to pull it free, but the whip tightened. The officer's eyes went wide and he let go of the grip in order to tear at the whip with both hands. A choking sound escaped him.

The guardcleric holding Charles rushed to assist his colleague, at the same time attempting to sheath his weapon. His hand suddenly turned, causing the blade to rise above the sheath. Somehow, it bent and twisted itself upward, piercing his body beneath his breastplate. Blood gushing over his hands, the shocked guard collapsed into his garrotted companion whose eyes bulged as he tried in desperation to hook his fingers inside the demonic noose. The pierced guard slumped next to Charles who stumbled away in shock. A second later the first officer let out a strangled gasp, and joined his companion. The whip still entwined around his throat.

'Robert!' called Constance from somewhere behind him. ''ware the others.' He glanced to his left to see the remaining WitchFinder guardclerics converging on his position. A part of Robert wanted to flee, but his fury dominated. He glared at the armed men, who had terrorised and murdered in the name of their holy sect.

One stumbled, his sword arm turned, the edge of his blade slashed through the throat of the guard next to him. Another gave out with a desperate cry as he slipped and fell into the pool of blood and innards. As he did, he dropped his weapon, which somehow tangled the feet of another guard. That man spun around, then hit the ground skull-first. There was an audible snap and the guardcleric stilled, his head twisted at an unnatural angle.

But now the rest of the guardclerics surrounded Robert, who eyed them as he would vermin that sought to devour his foodstuffs. In his mind they were no more than that. The woodsman's memory flashed back to the time he had discovered a sack of grain infested with rats. He had done the only thing that he could to keep the creatures from spreading. He had burned the sack. Burned it with the vermin still within.

BURNED THEM

The foremost guardcleric cried out. He dropped his sword and stared in horror at his hands as they began to blacken before the eyes of all. In a single breath, the flesh crisped, the muscle and sinew turned to ash. Even the bone darkened and darkened, until it burst into flames. Before a moment or two had passed, nothing remained of his hands.

As he ran about screaming, slapping his burning limbs against his body, the others began to suffer in like manner. The first guard burst into flames. His face shrivelling and his body shook, even his armour tarnished as if had been tossed into a wood-fuelled furnace. His screaming was cut short as his face began to disintegrate.

His face crumpled, his eyes melting into their sockets with a horrible finality. The burning black figure collapsed into a heap of bones that further smoked away to dust.

His comrades had no time to gape in fear at his fate, for they too were to perish in the same manner. Their cries were shrill and their deaths were marked by the clatter of empty armour and falling weapons.

Only after they all were smoking ash did Robert return to his senses, and stare at a monstrous sight, that he could still even now not fully link to himself. Yet neither could the woodsman deny the fiery urge that had swept through him, the urge that had focused on the hapless men.

An unnatural silence filled Gustenai.

Robert finally tore his gaze from the macabre remains and looked at his brother who stood but a few steps from him. Panting, still obviously in some pain from the harsh cutting lash of the whip, Charles gaped at his older sibling.

'Robert' he finally succeeded in whispering. But Robert was looking past Charles to where the remainder of the townsfolk still stood, packed together even though their tormentors were all dead. He saw no relief in their eyes, but only what the woodsman recognized as dread.

Dread of him.

Murmuring arose from within the group. When Robert stretched forth a hand toward them, his friends moved as one away from his touch. That, in turn, caused Robert to retreat a step. He looked around and saw that other townsfolk had stepped out from hiding. Faces he had known all his life now eyed him as the former prisoners had.

'I didn't do anything' he murmured, more to himself than others. 'I didn't do anything' the son of Dorian protested again, louder this time.

But the people of Gustenai saw him differently, he knew. They now believed that he had slaughtered all the clericguards. How could they not? Before their eyes, one man had been struck by lightning, another strangled by his own weapon, and the rest brought down in manners no one could ever claim to be natural.

Robert spotted Tiresta his friend since childhood. He stepped toward the owner of the Nag's Head. The old man had been as near a father to him, as anyone since the death of Dorian.

Tiresta would at least see sense.

The stout figure backed away, his stony expression not entirely hiding his revulsion and anxiety. He mutely shook his head. Someone tugged on his sleeve. Charles. Still wincing from the pain of his beating, his brother whispered, 'Robert, come away from here. Quickly!'

'I've got to make them see sense, Charles. They can't possibly believe.'

'They believe. I think even I believe. That doesn't matter. Look around. You're not Robert Dorianson to them anymore. You're the fiend that the Bishop's Master WitchFinder claimed you to be. That's all that they see.' Brow wrinkled tight, Robert glanced from one face to another. All he saw were the same dark emotions. Lockout reappeared and with him his nephew Downsword. The captain had his arm in a sling and there was a gash on his right cheek. Behind the pair came the men who had been ordered to lock up the captain in his own quarters.

Downsword was the one who finally spoke to Robert. 'Keep perfectly still. Don't do a damned thing, Robert, except put your hands behind you.'

'I'm not the cause of all this, I was getting married today,' the woodsman insisted, knowing all the while that his protests were as futile as ever. You have to listen to me.'

'Archers are positioned,' Lockout anxiously interrupted. 'Please listen to reason Robert.' The woodsman shook. No one would listen to him. He was surrounded by insanity. They saw in him a murderer, a monster. Distracted by his own turmoil, he almost did not notice a subtle motion by Downsword. The captain's words returned to him. Archers. Those who had once been his friends would rather kill him than understand his predicament.

'No!' Robert cried out. 'No!'

The ground shook. People toppled over. Something whistled past his ear. As the tremor overtook Gustenai a hand pulled Robert away. It was not Charles however, but Constance. 'This is our only chance. Come.' Unable, and unwilling to think anymore, he allowed her to guide him out of the town.

Although those around them seemed unable to keep their footing, neither the woodsman nor his bride had any difficulty. Someone shouted his name. Despite Constance's tugging, Robert looked back and saw Charles on all fours. His brother was trying to follow, but suffered the same problems as the rest of Gustenai.

Ignoring Constance's protest, he went back for Charles. Charles took his hand and suddenly found his footing. Holding tight, Robert led his brother from the chaos.

'Horses!' Charles shouted above the din. 'We need horses. 'Robert was about to argue that they had no time to secure even one animal let alone five, when suddenly a horse raced ahead of them. It was followed by several more, all bearing the saddles of the Church of Light. They raced directly towards the woods, straight into the waiting hands of Archer.

Skilled in dealing with animals, the hunter easily brought under control three of them. Yvetta managed to catch another, but a fifth skipped past her and escaped.

Robert paused before the hunter, the two lifelong friends reading much into each other's gazes. 'We must be away from here,' Archer finally said, thrusting the reins of two horses toward the woodsman. 'Away until they come to their senses.' But both men knew that such a thing would never happen. Archer and Yvetta could return, yes, and would if the bowman had his way. However, Robert and by fault of blood, Charles was likely saying good-bye to their home forever.

'We've only four mounts,' the trader's daughter gasped.

'Constance!' Screamed Robert, realising his bride no longer accompanied them, he looked back. His wife lay in the dust at the edge of the town, an arrow through her throat, still staring in his direction, but life and love no longer sparkled and twinkled in those beautiful green eyes.

Robert raised his hands above his head, his fists clenched. He began to scream, an anguished howl that began deep within his being. As he did so the entire town's buildings crumbled to dust.

Nothing remained but the body of his bride, his Constance.

~

I opened my eyes; and sat up with tears running down my cheeks. Was it a dream, or another memory of an ancient ancestor, someone like Robert the Meek?

THE BARQUE
Mother River

"SEKHI?"

"YES Q'REM," REPLIED THE BEAUTIFUL BLONDE WOMAN, sat with a large black cat curled on her lap. They sat in the front of the barque as it made its journey across the mighty river, across the cosmos dividing the worlds inhabited by the relatives of Ra, and the younger Earth wherein the children of Ra had initially been seeded.

"How long will I have been gone when we get back? I reckon somewhere around six or seven months."

"I cannot say truly, but I believe it will be closer to more than a year of your time."

"Oh my god... that's just not fair, my poor parents, they must think I'm dead, I just can't wait to see them again, will they still love me?"

"Fear not my dearest; they will love you, who could not?"

"Huh, shows how much you know about people."

"I have known a few, in fact quite a few more than a few, being worshiped does wonders for my complexion." Sekhemet replied in a sultry sexy voice, breaking the sombre mood.

Q'rem laughed out loud, causing the ferryman to pause and look. grinning broadly she quipped; "You are a real bad girl Sekhi, I feel sorry for our poor menfolk if you ever get your claws into them."

"What do you mean if?"

THE RETURN

There was a gentle crunch as the boat came to shore and ground across a bank of shingle, looking back the way they had come Q'rem could see the lights of the city on the opposite bank. In front of her a thick mist obscured all except the immediate surroundings. Sekhi jumped lightly to shore, the black cat remained on the goddess' shoulders throughout. With her free hand she reached to aid Q'rem. "Whist girl, I'm no old granny yet," she said and as nimbly as the blonde hopped the short distance to land.

Turning to the ferryman Q'rem called "Shokran!" That worthy poled away from shore without a backward glance, Q'rem watched him for a moment, *I wonder what happens now?* she thought, almost fearful of what she would find.

Sekhi had already begun to walk into the swiftly thinning mist, with a start Jeanne skipped after her, she glanced back once but the river had disappeared, only the plains remained. How did I know that was going to happen, she thought.

Over a gentle rise the lights and outline of the camp came into view, "I'm home," she said aloud, "Sekhi, how can we explain my being away?"

"But have you been away darling? We have returned to the exact same moment that you departed."

As they entered the township under the unseeing eyes of the sodjers, Q'rem could see the ropes of soup still waiting to fall into the expectant bowls. With an almost imperceptible snap everything began to move, the spell was broken.

"How will I explain my longer hair and my tanned skin?"

"Oh you'll think of something," replied the little blonde.

FORT BRIMAT

'What is it beloved?' Keysha's concern was palpable, 'Was it another of your dreams?'

Toana put her hand on my shoulder, 'I am not sure I like all these changes you have had, they seem overly hard for you to bear,' she sent.

'No, my loves, it's not difficult, just some times the regressions are sad and agonizing, when I realise just how tough their lives were.'

'How tough compared to ours' interjected Keysha.

'Tough, my sweet, ours is a different type of tough I guess, but, enough of my dreams, dwelling on them will not solve what happened or didn't happen, it was thousands of years ago.'

'Could you not help them? Could we not help them?' Toana asked.

'No my love, if we went back in time and our bodies were tangible we would probably be burnt at the stake for being witches, or killed for being different. Even if I went alone, it would be too much of a shock for them to see me, even without my purple skin and hair I am almost as dissimilar to them as you two are. Then there is the paradox,'

'A paradox, what is that?' asked Keysha,

'Travelling back in time has terrible contradictions, if it were possible for me, or for us to change anything, such as altering the outcomes whatever they might be, of my many times past ancestors. Then that change will affect me. So say my ancestor were to die before they had children, I would blink out of existence, it would be as if I, and all those who came before me following their death, had never been born.'

That is a frightening thought,' rumbled Toana, turning the concept over in her mind.

A thought broke into our conversation it was Lord Dominie, 'CHILDREN, GO YOU NOW TO FORT BRIMAT, Q'REM HAS NEED OF YOU.'

We rose, took a quick cold dip in the pool, and dressed ourselves in armour I had liberated from the depository at Castra's main exit. The girls were unable to wear helmets, what with big ears and big snouts, I joked when they asked if anything would fit. Toana wore one of the biggest suits we could find, Keysha though tall, was easier to accommodate. Mine was for a short trooper; such was the difference in stature between the original humans and three of us.

Once prepared, and with us suitably weaponised, I wrapped my arms around two Kevlar armoured waists, and jumped to Fort Brimat.

The Door slammed shut behind us...

END OF BOOK TWO

Thank you for ploughing your way through Book 2

Here it comes; **Book Three   ULRICH**

I enjoyed producing this next Book immensely, although it took a great deal of research and innovative (crazy) formation, to try and keep the whole historical fantasy/reality section from falling into the depths of GA-GA land.

A Baron, medieval knights and Gypsy magic, bring them all together and we have; Book Three, Which recounts the tale of Rob's time shifting ability, Rob with Sekhi's assistance, bring desperately required recruits to assist in the confrontation against the Shishmanid, or Adversary, as they are also known. Still lusting after the fertile and sparsely inhabited lands, the Shishmanid begin to intrude through the tear in greater numbers. Finally they assault in an overwhelming horde of many thousands. Assisted this time by the giant Anakim, they face the people of the 'New' world.

The forces of good and evil amongst the celestial powers begin to take sides.

It's not certain who will win...   IF ANYONE!

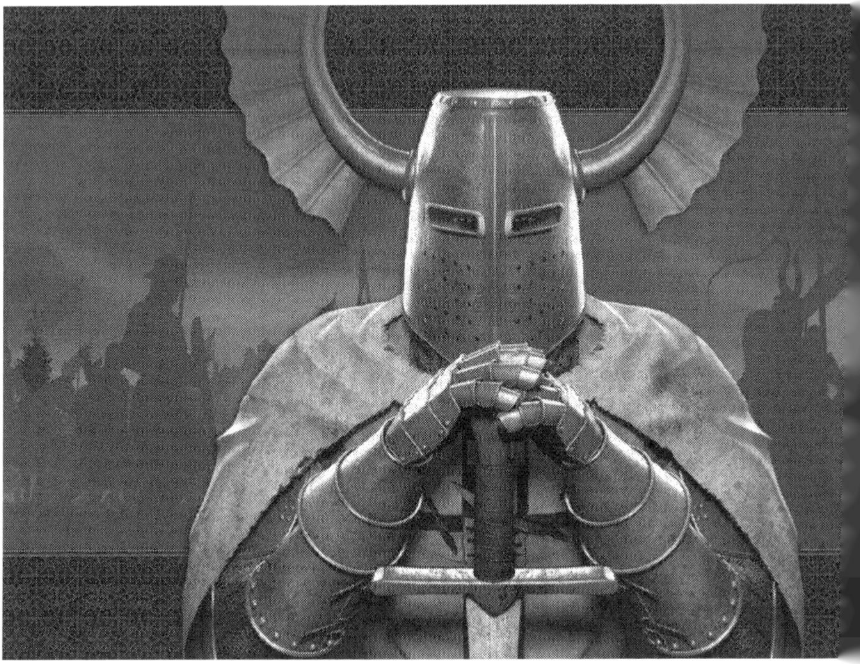

Printed in Great Britain
by Amazon